THEY CALL ME THE MERCENARY

#17

BUCKINGHAM BLOWOUT

Books by Jerry Ahern

The Survivalist Series
#1: Total War
#2: The Nightmare Begins
#3: The Quest
#4: The Doomsayer
#5: The Web
#6: The Savage Horde
#7: The Prophet

The Defender Series
#1: The Battle Begins
#2: The Killing Wedge
#3: Out of Control
#4: Decision Time
#5: Entrapment

They Call Me the Mercenary Series
#1: The Killer Genesis
#2: The Slaughter Run
#3: Fourth Reich Death Squad
#4: The Opium Hunter
#5: Canadian Killing Ground
#6: Vengeance Army
#7: Slave of the Warmonger
#8: Assassin's Express
#9: The Terror Contract
#10: Bush Warfare
#11: Death Lust!
#12: Headshot!
#13: Naked Blade, Naked Gun
#14: The Siberian Alternative
#15: The Afghanistan Penetration
#16: China Bloodhunt
#17: Buckingham Blowout

THEY CALL ME THE MERCENARY

#17

BUCKINGHAM BLOWOUT

JERRY AHERN

SPEAKING VOLUMES, LLC
NAPLES, FLORIDA
2013

THEY CALL ME THE MERCENARY
BUCKINGHAM BLOWOUT #17

ISBN 978-1-61232-237-7

For Don Tope—good fan, good friend. . . .

Chapter One

The sounds woke Frost up. Noises from a long way off.

He opened his eye. The sounds were coming from him. He closed his eye.

Frost willed himself to be quiet, then the sounds—groans—stopped.

He opened his eye again. There was nothing to see. In front of him was darkness and black. There was nothing to—but then he blinked and the world became less dark and took on shades of murky gray. He blinked again and his eye came into focus. His face was against a brick wall.

A wall for what? he wondered, and when he tried turning his head to see he started groaning again. He stopped moving. He took a deep breath. His chest and rib cage ached. More groans. His body, from head to toe, felt tender, sore—abused.

The one-eyed man ran his tongue over his teeth, half expecting to discover they were broken or had been kicked out altogether. They hadn't been either.

"Thank God for small favors," he mumbled, the voice behind the words reaching his ears not sounding familiar.

"Ignore the pain," he rasped, shifting his weight and rolling onto his back, keeping his eye open, gently rocking his head from side to side. He couldn't ignore the pain. To his left was the brick wall he'd been facing, stretching straight up for what he guessed was more than sixty feet.

Over to his right it seemed much the same—another brick wall disappearing into the night sky, a single back-lit window on the wall about ten yards up. The walls were too close together for a street. He decided he must be in some kind of alley.

"An alley—an alley? What alley?"

Frost rolled onto his hands and knees and tried to stand. Yellow and green floaters danced across his eye, a sharp spasm of pain filled his head. "Shit," he murmured. Bracing his palms against the wall to his right, he made it to his feet. Reasonably certain he wasn't going to fall, he pushed away from the wall and stood there, swaying, back and forth, getting his balance.

Frost shivered. There was a fine spray of mist hanging in the air, forcing a chill up along his spine. His clothes were saturated and heavy with water—he glanced to his feet. He had been sprawled in the center of a puddle. His jacket was torn and the front of his shirt was splotched with oil. The insides of his shoes felt squishy and there was a hole the size of his fist over the knee in the left leg of his trousers.

"Wonderful."

On his feet. Aware of his surroundings.

Frost noticed something some distance away. Beyond the alley—cars, trucks, funny-looking buses, crowds of people. "A big city," he rasped. A city, a large one, with each noise overlapping the other.

Frost thought the best thing to do was to find his way home, change into some clean clothes. . . .

The one-eyed man frowned. Going home to change? Home was—where was home?

"Damnit," he muttered, running his hand over his face, his fingers stopping as they brushed across an eye patch. He closed his right eye and lifted the patch away, then dropped the patch back into place. He was blind in his left eye—and there wasn't even an eye there? Where was it? The eye?

Hands groping through the pockets of his sodden jacket and trousers, Frost searched for a wallet, a checkbook, a passport—something with a name. There was nothing with a name.

No identification.

"OK," he whispered to himself. The voice wasn't familiar—but it had to be his. "Leave the alley—maybe I'll find something."

He had two options. He could leave the alley by going to his left—there were vehicles moving along a street adjacent to the alley—or he could leave to the right. Down that way, the butt end of the alley was lost in shadows, obscured by gray drizzle.

"Left." Out to the street and then a quick trip to the nearest police station. Going to the authorities could be a mistake—for all he knew he could be a wanted man. But something convinced him he wasn't a criminal, and that going to the police would do him more good than harm.

Turning to his left, Frost started walking, his steps unsure at first until, gradually, he realized he wasn't going to fall. He shivered again and pulled his soaked coat tighter around his chest. He felt chilled to the bone and there was a pounding inside his head that refused to go away. Still, he was on his feet and sorting out his problems. Very soon now, the answers would—

Frost lurched to a halt. A big, black sedan. It screeched across the entrance to the alley, blocking his way, rocking with the suddenness of the stop.

"There he is!" a man from the passenger side shouted. He pointed a long, bony finger at Frost. "We got 'im now!"

The sedan was still shivering on its shocks as the car's doors popped open and four men poured out, the pair storming from the back seat looking like deformed bookends—that similar.

Without waiting for his pals to follow, the man who had first spotted Frost, the one from the front passenger seat, tore down the alley, drawing a knife from a sheath at his belt, wildly slashing the long, green, glinting blade back and forth as he charged.

Frost stood his ground, uncertain. That the man with the knife racing toward him meant to kill him was obvious. Exactly why he had been singled out as victim-for-the-night, the one-eyed man had no idea.

As Frost watched the knife-wielding assassin close the distance between them he noticed his would-be killer's three friends were bringing up the rear—each apparently content to let their eager partner have some fun with easy slaughter. The man was thirty feet away. Twenty. Ten, then five—the blade stabbed out at Frost's unprotected chest.

When the point of the knife plowed through the space where Frost's heart was supposed to be, the one-eyed man was no longer there. Side-stepping the attack with— Frost thought surprisedly—a beautifully timed maneuver to the right, Frost felt himself grin with satisfaction as the knife passed harmlessly through empty air—throwing the man behind the knife totally off balance.

Before the knife-wielder could recover, Frost—instinctively—spun on his right foot, moving counterclockwise, swinging his left leg around, then made a kick to the middle of the killer's back with his left heel. There was a grunt of pain, the sound of something—ribs?—cracking, and the man started to fall. Pivoting clockwise on his right foot, the one-eyed man swung his left foot up, delivering a high, sweeping kick to the side of the staggering man's head. The man moaned, then sank like a pile of dirty laundry to the slick alley pavement.

"All right!" Frost laughed. "Way to go!" His defense against the man with the knife had come naturally to him, as if facing an armed foe was something he was trained to handle on a day-to-day basis. Frost looked down, searching for the man's knife, but the blade was nowhere to be seen. And there wasn't any time for him to hunt for it, either, he realized. His other three enemies were closing in fast—two of them producing wooden clubs from beneath their jackets; the third man, the one who'd been driving the sedan, was bringing out a knife.

"Holy shit!" Frost rasped.

He wheeled on his heels and ran.

"Cor, Rob, he's gettin' away!" the voice shouted from behind him, the words ringing down the alley with a strong British accent.

"Keep your hair on, little brother," another voice called, in an accent just as pronounced. "He's as good as ours."

Frost glanced behind him quickly, the three men eating up the distance separating them. The one-eyed man raced for the dubious exit at the opposite end of the alley. It was still too dark for him to see that far, but he was betting his life on the hope that it wasn't a dead end. Puddles splashed and sprayed around him as his feet pounded the slippery alleyway surface, driving him forward in a headlong lunge, the sounds of the men chasing him fueling the energy of his flight.

Up ahead to his left, an old woman opened a door onto the alley, curiously staring out.

"Please!" Frost called to the woman, knowing that if he could make it through the door and put it between himself and his attackers, then his odds for surviving the next few minutes would greatly increase. "Don't close the—"

But even as the words left his mouth the woman—frightened or uninterested, he didn't know which—slammed the door shut in Frost's face. Wasting precious seconds, Frost tried the door. It was locked. "Shit!" He turned and continued his run down the alley.

The drizzle was falling heavier now, filling the alley with banging sounds as the raindrops drummed trash can lids he ran past, the rain drenching Frost's already soaked clothes, weighing him down still more. Then he was at the alley's end and panting to catch his breath. He faced a solid brick wall more than fifty feet high. "A damn dead end." There was a narrow gate six feet tall off to his right, but there was no time to investigate to see where it might lead. Instead, Frost twisted completely around and pressed his back to the wall, waiting for the men chasing him to make their move. Only now that they supposedly had him cornered, none of the killers appeared to be in much of a hurry.

"Watch his feet, Harry," the youngest-seeming of the pair carrying the wooden clubs warned the guy with the knife. "Ya saw what he did to Martin."

"Yeah, I saw," Harry said. "An' I wasn't impressed. Now, stand aside while me and my knife carve this geezer up right."

Frost waited. The men with the clubs fell back. Harry, the one gripping the switchblade in his right hand, jockeyed forward into position.

"Awright, pal," Harry laughed. "'At's it for you."

Harry came for him, a backhand slash Frost guessed was designed to rip out his stomach. There was nothing to do but rely on unremembered instincts again to save his life—side-stepping, feigning a kick, chopping down with the knife edge of his left hand on the killer's right wrist, snapping the wrist, breaking it, the oversize switch-blade flying from Harry's grasp as the killer started to scream. Frost choked off the scream by spreading the thumb of his right hand away from his fingers and whipping the hollow edge he'd created into his attacker's throat. Harry sputtered and spit blood as Frost, digging his fingers like a claw into the man's throat, slammed Harry around against the brick wall and to the ground, finishing him off with a fatal kick to the back of the skull.

Frost bent down and flashed Harry's discarded switch-blade into his hand, just as the men armed with the wooden clubs separated so they could come at him from opposite directions. The one-eyed man shook water from his eye and smiled. Taking out the first hood with the knife hadn't been a fluke—what was left of Harry proved that. And the way he'd disposed of the second man with a knife only added to his conviction that his success so far had to be the end result of years of rigorous training. A man with less experience would already be dead, he reasoned. Which made him . . . what? Some kind of professional killer? Frost didn't know, and at the moment all he could hope was that he would live long enough to find out.

Standing alert, in a guard stance—his body turned sideways, with his left foot stationed in front of his right—the one-eyed man motioned with the fingers of his right hand, taunting the men he faced to make their move. "What are ya assholes waitin' for? An invitation?"

The man to Frost's left almost growled, raised his club then leaped, simultaneously bringing the bar-shaped weapon down in a blow aimed at Frost's head.

As the club descended, Frost's hands, crossed at the wrists, blocked the downswing at the forearm, deflecting the strike, Frost's right foot snapped up into the groin, causing the man to lose his stability, to fall back. Frost wheeled, making a rapid back kick with his left foot to the side, slamming the man just above the hip, sending him stumbling back and against the legs of the second man with a club. The snarling pair were on their way to the ground as Frost wheeled to his left and ran for the gate, tugging as hard as he could on its handle.

It was locked.

The men with the clubs were clambering to their feet as Frost grabbed for the top of the six-foot gate and jumped, hauling himself up and getting halfway over when one of the clubs slammed across his back, knocking him sailing through the air to the opposite side of the gate. He skidded on his feet, then to his knees, scraping his left hand on one of the walls to keep from sprawling.

He was up, stumbling, staggering—running.

He looked behind him. The pair after his life were wrapping their five-pound, ham-sized hands around the top of the gate and physically ripping it off its hinges. It

12

took little imagination for Frost to picture what those hands would do if they got hold of his body. The upper half of the gate was beginning to break apart. Frost turned down a narrow passage, less than a yard wide, which ran between two of the buildings forming the end of the alley to his rear.

There was a crashing sound and a quick glance over his shoulder showed Frost that the club-armed duo had broken through the gate and were once more after him.

With the echo of fast footfalls following his own, Frost charged along the space between the buildings, speeding down the concrete passageway as it angled sharply to the right, then continuing on as it opened up onto a straight-away leading to a street.

"Feets don't fail me now," he panted, and then he was clear of the buildings, out in the open, slipping across a rain-slicked sidewalk, pushing through a crowd of pedestrians, hearing their shouts and screams and curses as he shoved them aside, reaching a curb, checking to the left for traffic, seeing it was safe, and then bolting into the street—directly into the path of an oncoming double-decker monster of a red bus barreling down on him from the right.

Frost saw the bus out of the corner of his eye, tensed his legs and then leaped—women screaming, brakes on the bus screeching, the driver of the bus riding the horn—as the right front headlight on the double-decker brushed Frost's rear end. Frost was airborne, feeling his feet leave the ground, flying, then dropping, diving for the street, hitting it, rolling into his fall with his left shoulder, tumbling, and then back on his feet again.

Traffic along the street was at a standstill. The driver of the bus had stopped it in the middle of the road and was climbing out into the downpour. Frost's teeth were chattering together, either from his soaked condition or else from the shock of getting hit by the bus and miraculously surviving the accident—he couldn't decide the reason he liked best as he got to his feet.

He was pulling himself back together and checking to make sure no bones were broken when he saw the men who were trying to kill him emerge in a rush from the passage out of the alley. Both men jerked their heads left and right, looking for him he knew. With the bus driver, various pedestrians, and curious motorists converging on him, it was like shooting up a flare to attract their attention.

He could just make out the taller of the two point excitedly in his direction. Car horns were honking and the crowd was closing in on him in an ever-tightening circle as the club-wielders began a loping run across the street.

Frost shook himself free of a hand clutching his shoulder and began forcing his way up the sidewalk as, behind him, one of his adversaries suddenly shouted, "Stop the bastard—a child molester he is!" The words filling the wet night air couldn't have been any louder if they'd come from a bullhorn, Frost thought.

His mind raced, the sea of once-concerned faces belonging to the bus driver, pedestrians, and the motorists instantly changed—anger, hatred. Eyes that wanted blood. Most of those surrounding him drew back; the one exception was a transparent plastic raincoated boy with a shaved head, wearing blue jeans held up by suspenders, and dark black combat boots. About twenty-one, Frost guessed as the boy produced a knife from somewhere. Frost twisted right, hurling himself almost to the sidewalk, his hands and right foot balancing his weight, his left foot kicking out at the same time, driving into the gut of the glory-seeking youth before the knife could cut. There was a moan and the one-eyed man was up and moving, a spray of vomit just missing him as the boy doubled forward. But it gave Frost the opening he needed to make his move—breaking away from the crowd and rushing up the sidewalk. The two men who had been chasing him were less than thirty feet behind him as he looked back. And he had lost the knife when the bus hit him.

"Go for broke." Frost reached the end of the block, skidded around the deserted corner and stopped, waiting, pressing his body to the window front of a closed bakery, holding his breath, listening for sounds of his pursuers' shoes smacking against the wet sidewalk as they ran. The one-eyed man counted softly to himself.

"One, two, three, four . . ." he counted.

The first man rounded the corner. The one-eyed man lashed out—turning hard to the left, his right leg climbing, seeking the target, finding it, the instep of his right foot arcing high in a hooking kick to the front of the man's throat.

Immediately, there was a noise like a gargle, blood spraying from the mouth, both hands reaching for the throat, the club in the man's right hand slipping from his fingers. Frost caught the club as it fell, then swung its top-heavy end over and down, smashing the already dying man across the bridge of the nose. Chips of bone or cartilage—mingled with blood—sprayed from the man's nostrils as the body fell forward.

Shoving the toppling body aside with his left hand, Frost wheeled right in time—the second man was round-

15

house swinging his club at head level. Frost's borrowed club locked with it, the heel of the one-eyed man's left hand straight-arming forward and right into the man's right cheekbone. Frost's left wrist screamed at him. The man sagged, his club flying like a wooden rocket through the bakery window. At the sound of a small explosion, glass showered the sidewalk, shards of it showering Frost like the pouring rain.

The man sagged back, his left hand pushing back the jacket, grabbing for a gun in the waistband of his pants.

"Eat this!" Frost snarled, falling against the man, hacking with the club like a machete—the mouth, the nose, the forehead, the skull. Frost slumped back—the face beneath him was a pulp. Frost pushed himself up, heaved forward and retched.

The gun the man had been reaching for. Throwing away the wooden club he no longer needed, Frost bent over and lifted the pistol from the body, wiping the blood and vomit from it, hefting its weight into his hand. The shape of the gun's butt was oddly familiar in his hand. Holding the thing up to the glow of a nearby street lamp, he squinted to determine the make and model of the gun. It was a Browning High Power.

Slipping the pistol inside the waistband of his trousers, Frost turned into the night. Questions ran through his mind. No answers—just questions.

Chapter Two

Frost wandered—aimlessly was the word for it—for more than an hour, reflecting that people rarely wandered purposefully. He moved along avenues with names like Back Church Lane, Commercial Road, and Gunthorpe Street—walking north, south, left and right, sometimes actually making progress, but as often as not simply traveling in circles. The rain had quit falling not more than fifteen minutes earlier, but a harsh wind, tearing through his soggy clothes like he might just as well have been naked, racked him with chills more deep felt than before.

The one-eyed man had decided that he was in England, or more particularly, the sprawling city of London. The accents of the men who had attacked and tried to kill him, the double-decker bus that had struck him, the miserable weather that assaulted him.

"London."

The realization confused him even more. Try as he might, he could recall nothing to account for being in Great Britain. Neither that nor how he had happened to find himself waking up in an alley, or how the would-be killers had discovered him. Why had they wanted to kill him? And every time he did think he was on the verge of remembering something important, pain—blinding, burning—would erupt at the back of his head, pulling that something important away, beyond reach.

Since defeating the last of his attackers and taking the man's gun—the Browning High Power—Frost had spoken to no one. Once, three men in their early twenties, basically carbon copies of the shaven-headed young man Frost had been forced to take down near the accident with the bus earlier in the evening, laughing apparently over some private joke, had stepped across the sidewalk Frost was on, barring his advance. He had swung his suit coat open, halted only long enough for the trio to see the High Power worn inside his trouser band. They had walked on.

All about him as he rambled up and down the neighborhood streets, there was seemingly abject poverty, like a strong smell permeating the entire crowded, gray section of the city. Nowhere was there a single detached family dwelling to be seen. And if there were a common thread, he thought, a thread running through the various buildings he passed, it was that they all seemed to have been constructed as packaging for some now-defunct cracker manufacturer, one package calling for cramming as much into as tiny a structure as possible, the structures jammed one against the other, in space smaller than what might humanly be possible. The one-eyed man likened it to being in the exact middle of the world's largest prison yard, but with the walls surrounding the prisoners invisible walls—crime, malnutrition, ignorance.

18

Frost rounded a corner and moved onto a street whose sign read Bethnal Green Road—a reasonably sized thoroughfare reminding him of . . . what? Again the fragile connection linking what he saw to whatever forgotten memory he could almost remember faded before he could fully understand it. He rubbed at the pain at the back of his head. He kept on walking.

Midway down the block he was on, Frost could see where a group of people, perhaps as many as ten, mostly male, were lined up single file alongside a building, for some reason seeming to be waiting to get in. As he watched, two men exited the building, allowing the first two people in the line to vanish inside at the same time. Four such rotations took place before Frost came near enough to the building to smell it—food.

"Food," Frost said, licking his lips, walking faster, the scent masking the wet garbage odor of the street, filling the air, making his stomach rumble, his dry mouth water. When he'd last eaten or what that meal had been were some more things he could not remember.

The banner outside and above the building's front door read, Women's Volunteer Service Group. The windows were white curtained and thick with steam, and the harsh wind he'd been fighting since the rain had let up seemed somehow less severe as he stopped at the end of the line.

"Food?" Frost inquired of the person ahead of him.

The man—white haired, toothless, obviously aged, yet somehow ageless—merely nodded.

"How much?"

"Nuffin'," the white-haired old man replied. Frost thought of the word, cockney. It was, somehow, the way the man sounded. "Hit's on the 'ouse."

19

A free meal, Frost waited in line for it, looking at his wrist but seeing no watch, only a band of flesh lighter than that above or below it. But then it was his turn to go inside, the old man with him, then drifting off. It was the modern-day equivalent of a Depression-style soup kitchen, he thought. But then, he asked himself, how did he know that?

First he was greeted at the door by a plump grandmother-type woman who showed him where he could wash his hands before dining. His hands scrubbed with gritty, powdered soap and dried on brown paper towels that smelled when they became wet, Frost then took up a tray and stood in another line. He shuffled his way forward. "Chow line." He thought of what he said—what was that? He was given a plate piled high with stewed cabbage and boiled potatoes, a hard roll with yellow margarine, a helping of bright green hard peas. There was a mug of tea—it smelled like sweat tobacco—"Tobacco?" Milk was in it and he'd watched as two cubes of sugar had been added.

Frost left the serving area and carried his tray and meal to the end of one of the tan-painted hall's five long, folding dining tables, taking a seat in a folding wooden chair. Immediately—almost obsessively—he began devouring the food. He had just finished the last of his milky-sweet tea when a voice off to his right caught his attention.

A woman—she turned toward him.

"Would you care for some more?" she asked.

He felt something below his belt twitch.

Frost turned in his seat to face her. She was elegant—that was the word, he thought. Auburn hair—like

20

something alive of its own, framing her face, brushed back from her forehead. The hair was casual, unlike the clothing—it was expensive. Light tan—he thought the color was called beige—the skirt just below the knees, the blouse long-sleeved and silk. His eye was drawn back to her face—the eyes were an almost liquid dark brown. She walked toward him on high heels—but without them he judged she'd be at least five foot seven.

"I asked if you would care for some more—tea, I mean." She held up an aluminum teapot. "What's your pleasure?"

For the first time that day, Frost laughed. "Yes—more tea. I'll have more tea—please."

The woman nodded and reached for Frost's mug. "You're an American?"

The one-eyed man nudged the mug within range of the teapot. "Yeah, I guess I am. From the sounds of it—so are you."

"Sure am." She smiled again, tilting the spout of the pot over his mug, filling it to the brim.

"Thanks." Frost took the mug back. "So tell me— what's a good-looking American woman like you doing in the middle of . . . wherever it is we are?"

"Bethnal Green," she told him.

"Same as the name on the road outside," he added. "Still part of London, though?"

"Um-hmm."

"Good—at least I got that right." Frost sipped his tea, enjoying the burning sensation in his throat and stomach. "Good tea."

"Thank you." The woman—Frost pegged her as being a few years on the lean side of forty—excused herself to refill the cups of some of the other men. She came back, though, a few minutes later.

"Do you mind if I sit down for a minute?"

The one-eyed man shrugged. "Be my guest."

She set the teapot—it clanged empty—on the table, then took a folding chair directly across from him. "I don't remember seeing you in here before."

"That makes two of us," he smiled. "I don't remember ever being in here before."

"How did you happen to find your way to us this evening?"

"Walked," Frost informed her matter-of-factly, his right hand impulsively fumbling at the inside pocket of his coat—for a pack of cigarettes? He knew they weren't there. He felt himself frown, letting his hand drop away from his coat, then drank more of his tea. "I walked here tonight. And before you ask—no, I don't know for sure where it was I walked here from. To tell ya the truth, other than the fact that I'm an American, and that I'm in London, right now I don't know much about anything."

"Are you," she appeared to be weighing the impact of her words. "Are you in some kind of trouble?"

"Some kind of trouble—yeah. What kind of trouble . . . well, I'm still working on that one." And then because the very pretty woman with the soft eyes sitting across from him now seemed genuinely interested and because he realized talking was what he needed, Frost told her everything, confiding in her without hesitation, detailing all that had happened to him since regaining conscious-ness in the alley. The woman listened in total silence—Frost was unsure if it was because she was simply being courteous, or else because she thought he was insane and

22

didn't believe a single word he said.

He finished talking, not feeling much better for it, and drank the rest of his tea. It was cold now. "I don't know who I am, where I came from, what I'm doing in England, or how the hell I got to London. What I do know is that somebody out there dislikes me enough to send four guys out looking to polish me off." He frowned once more, feeling frustrated and helpless. "If I could maybe remember my name, then maybe the rest of this mess would start to fall into place."

"We're not totally in the dark as to your background," the woman smiled. "Your clothes, for example, they tell an awful lot."

Frost agreed. "Yeah—that I lie down in alleys," he laughed.

"No," she smiled, shaking her head. "More than that." Her brown eyes drifted over him, and she was watching his face now. "Your clothes may not look like much in their present condition, but when they were new I'm sure you didn't buy them in some bargain basement sale. They were expensive. And knowing they were tells us something else—you must not be poor. If you were, you couldn't afford to own the clothes you have on."

"That makes sense," Frost said. "It's gratifying knowing I don't always dress like this. I was starting to get worried."

"We're not out of the woods yet," she cautioned. "Back to your story for a second—do you have any proof that what you've told me is true?"

"Nope," Frost shrugged, thinking that maybe he had made a mistake being so open with the woman. "I can talk all night about how I hurt and ache and that if I hadn't been lucky as hell earlier, you wouldn't be sitting talkin' to me now. I can do all the talkin' in the world, but if you're convinced I'm wacko, that's all there is to it." He leaned in over the table, speaking low so only she could hear. "All I can do is keep repeating what I already told you—a couple of hours ago four crazies I can't remember ever seeing before tried murdering me. I think maybe I killed at least three of 'em. I'm not positive. I do know that when it was all over I wound up with something I didn't have in the beginning." He pushed away from the table, standing and pulling back the bottom of his coat so that the Browning High Power was visible for an instant. Then he sat down again. "This gun I'm carrying is real, kid."

"No doubt about that," the woman smiled strangely. "Do you know how to use it?"

Frost answered automatically. "Not sure, but I suppose so. I imagine it would be pretty much like taking on those four guys who were tryin' to kill me. When I had to survive, my instincts took over and I did OK. Somehow, I think it'd be the same with the gun."

"Have you thought about going to the police?"

"For about this long," Frost returned, demonstrating by snapping his fingers. "But until I can remember more about me, or else get a handle on who it is that's trying to kill me, I can't see myself running open-armed to the law. I gotta be suspicious of everyone."

"Including me?" the woman asked suddenly.

"For you, kid—well, maybe I'll make an exception."

"Glad to hear it." She reached her right hand across the table. "The name's Monica Hewlett-Jones. We'll work on your name later." Frost took her right hand for

24

an instant—it was warm, soft. Then Monica stood up from the table. "Hold on a minute while I get my coat."

Frost's eye opened wide. "And then what?"

"Then—I take you home with me. Unless you have a better idea?"

"Not really," the one-eyed man smiled.

Chapter Three

It was a forty-minute drive, she'd said, from the Women's Volunteer Service Group charity dining hall in Bethnal Green to her apartment in Chelsea. The car was old—really old. A Rover.

"Snazzy wheels," Frost grinned, nothing else to say. He sat in the passenger seat on the left side of the car, admiring the detail-work of the wood-inlaid dash, his right hand running over the fine leather texture of the Rover's custom upholstery. "Corinthian leather?" She laughed. "Must've cost a bundle restoring it," he said.

"The Rover's not restored," Monica answered. He could see the faint edge of her smile. "It's been in my husband's family since the day it was showroom fresh."

Frost tilted the vent of the heater so that more of the warm air was hitting his face. "You're married, then?"

"I was. Jonathan died in an accident eleven months ago."

"I'm sorry to hear that," Frost offered. "I don't know if I'm married or if I ever was—but losing someone you love. It'd be tough."

"It was—is—will be, I suppose, really." She cleared her throat. "I was devastated knowing Jonathan was lost to me forever. For the first six months I lived like a hermit. I didn't want to go anywhere, do anything, or talk to anyone. I was numb on life. Then, finally, one morning I took a good look at myself in the mirror and got worried as hell. My hair was a mess, the bags under my eyes could've been used for grocery sacks, and my face looked all puffy and swollen. It really scared me, so much so that I made up my mind then and there to quit feeling sorry for myself and put my life back in order. It was shortly after that when I volunteered to help out twice a week with the meal giveaway program in Bethnal Green. I miss him just as much—and it really isn't any easier. But—well, like you with those four men in the alley. I guess I knew how to survive, too."

"Coming from America," Frost began lamely. "Hell—you must have some relatives you could have turned to. Did you ever think about moving back?"

"Not even once. England's my home, has been for the past nine years. I love it here. I could never think of leaving." She held the wheel with her right hand while slipping her left into the top of her purse, the bag resting on the seat between them. "Do you object if I smoke?"

"Not unless you mind some company. I've been wanting a cigarette since dinner."

Monica retrieved a slim, gold cigarette case with matching butane lighter, holding them out for Frost to take. "They're menthol."

"Maybe I like menthol," Frost said, flipping open the case and removing two cigarettes. "What brand are they?"

"Dunhill's."

"Maybe it's my favorite. Want me to light yours?"

"Thank you—yes."

Frost did, placing the filter tips of both cigarettes between his lips, then working the striking wheel on the lighter, easing his thumb down on the gas lever. A miniature flame shot from the end of the lighter and he fed the end of each cigarette into its center. He inhaled, saw the tobacco catch, and then passed one of the cigarettes to Monica. "Just decided—maybe I don't like menthol after all." His eye fixed suddenly, almost hypnotically, on the flickering flame of the lighter, his mind straining, stretching to comprehend the significance of why he found the lighter's flame so fascinating. Then it came to him—a single word, a solitary link with his mysterious past. Frost felt like a child taking his first unassisted step and he couldn't help himself. He laughed out loud.

"What's so funny?" Monica asked, a startled sound rising in her voice.

"I'm happy," he told her. "It's your cigarette lighter—using it triggered the only positive memory I've had all day." He inhaled the menthol-based smoke deep into his lungs again, then slowly exhaled. "I remembered what kind of lighter it is I usually carry—a Zippo. I usually carry a battered old Zippo lighter; and I actually remembered it!"

"Congratulations!"

"Yeah," Frost smiled, "at this rate—a clue a day—I should have a solid peg on knowing who I really am by the middle of the next century."

Monica's home on Royal Avenue in London's "fashionable"—she had used that word—Chelsea was scarcely the apartment Frost had expected. It had an impressive cornice-decorated ceiling just inside the entrance way, a long, wood-banistered staircase leading to the second floor, subdued indirect lighting, polished oak hardwood floors, and imported Indian carpets visible throughout— Frost was impressed.

"A tour of the apartment can wait, I think. Right now I'm pointing you in the direction of the shower upstairs so you can shave and clean up. Fresh towels are in the linen cupboard just outside the bathroom door. You'll find disposable razors and shaving cream in the medicine cabinet, plus a bar of new soap on the tray beneath the sink. We've got plenty of hot water, so don't be afraid of turning the taps on as warm as you like. Have I forgotten anything?"

Frost nodded. "Clothes—after I strip outta these, ahh . . ." He let it hang.

"There's a clean robe that should fit you hanging from a hook on the wall next to the shower."

"A clean robe?" Frost mused. "And one that should fit me? It's almost like you knew I'd be here tonight."

"Not really," Monica reassured him. "But it doesn't hurt to be prepared." And she smiled.

He had washed his body, washed his hair—then done each twice more. He stood now, the warm spray pelting him, staring at the gray hairs on his chest. He wondered—suddenly—how old he was. He turned the water to straight cold and gave up caring.

He wiped the steam away from the bathroom mirror, the reflection of the face staring back belonging to the same stranger he had seen when he'd shaved.

"Couldn't wake up in the body of a handsome prince— no," Frost told his reflection, the finger tips of his left hand brushing lightly over the scar where his left eye should have been. He searched through the archives of his memory. How had his eye been lost? All he could come up with was an endless string of nonsense reasons, involving everything from taffy to chopsticks, and none of it making any sense—and all the jokes were bad.

Sometime during his shower Monica had apparently slipped into the bathroom unnoticed and left him a new-seeming pair of blue pajamas. They were on the corner of the bathroom's marble-topped sink. "Amazing," Frost observed, trying on the bottoms, finding they fit perfectly. He left the top.

He eased his eye patch into place and pulled on the terrycloth bathrobe Monica had provided. Like the pajamas, the robe fit like it had been hand-tailored. And like the pajamas, it was blue. "Here's looking at you, kid," he curtly informed his reflection, then exited the bathroom to go find Monica. He heard kitchen noises from the floor below and homed in on them. She was fixing food, turned to face him and, wiping her hands on an apron, smiled.

"So, that's what you look like. Not bad at all." She looked to be putting the finishing touches to broiled steak and grilled onions. "I couldn't help noticing how you wolfed down the cabbage and the potatoes at the dining hall tonight, so I thought you might appreciate something more substantial to eat."

"Smells delicious. And, yeah—you're right." Frost crossed to a leather-covered bar stool and took a seat. "Thanks for the jammies—they fit just fine."

"You're welcome. How do you like your steak?"

"Right at this moment a step this side of moo oughta do it," he smiled.

"What a rare sense of taste," Monica laughed. She put the steak onto a plate she had been warming in the oven,

30

topping the meat with a towering pile of grilled onions. "One steak a step this side of moo," she announced. "Is here in the breakfast nook OK?"

"Terrific."

He took the plate and began eating his way through his second meal of the evening, a far more pleasurable one than number one. He ate slowly, drinking through an ice-cold bottle of Watney's beer—light, dry, coppery-amber hued.

Because he had already revealed what little information he knew regarding himself and his background, Frost was content to listen while he ate as Monica related, in her soft, soothing voice, certain facts about her past which she wanted him to know.

"Jonathan originally was an executive director with the British Foreign Service," she suddenly said, as if uncorking something inside of her. "He graduated Eton and Cambridge." She licked her lips. "He had been in the U.S. heading up a recruiting program—they wanted to secure qualified technical advisors for Great Britain's North Sea oil ventures. That's when he and I—well, when we met. I was a secretary to one of the vice presidents with Standard Oil of California. It was what you called a whirlwind love affair—just a single week.

"By the end of that week," Monica smiled, "I was hopelessly—I really mean the word hopelessly—in love. Jonathan was due to return to the U.K. and I was heartbroken. And if Jonathan hadn't been too stubborn to admit it, so was he. I saw him off at the airport, we said our goodbyes, and then I cried myself all the way home.

"The phone was ringing in the front room when I got in, and when I went over to answer it, it was Jonathan on the other end of the line—phoning me from his flight. It was somewhere over Canada by then. That's when he proposed and that's when I accepted. Twelve days later I flew to London and we were married.

"Jonathan had said his family had money, but we never really talked about it. It wasn't until I was in England and we were back together that I discovered how extremely wealthy his family really was. And then so was I. We stayed here most of the time—we were here just before he, ahh," and she cleared her throat.

"We have a place in Surrey—just like you see in the movies—with servants, horses, hunting dogs—not necessarily in that order," and she forced a smile.

Frost drained the last of the Watney's from his glass, then set the tumbler down on the table, feeling a broad smile settling over his face. "If you don't mind my saying so—that was a damn good dinner. Jonathan was a lucky man."

"He used to tell me that. He was sort of like you—without looking like you, I mean. I, ahh—I guess maybe that's why when you looked like you needed help back there, I, ahh . . ." and she let it hang.

"What kind of accident was it?" Frost asked her.

"Hit and run," she answered, looking down at her plate. "They never caught the man responsible."

"Sorry's a stupid thing to say, I guess."

"Not if it's sincere," she smiled. Frost thought he detected tears in her eyes.

Frost started to say something, but a chorus of musical chimes cut him off. "What's the hell's that?"

"Company. I hope you won't get angry, but while you were in the shower, I telephoned a friend and asked him to stop by."

32

Frost's eye narrowed. "This friend of yours with the police?"

"Don't be silly." Monica stood up from the table as the musical chimes from the doorbell rang again. "My friend's a doctor. I should warn you, though—he's quite fond of the American West."

The friend's name was Dr. Frank Titchen—a mild-mannered-seeming man in his early sixties, Frost guessed, standing about five-and-a-half feet tall, and carrying the ubiquitous black bag of his profession. He wore an ankle-length raincoat—which Monica assisted him in removing—under which he wore razor-edged, creased black trousers, and an ornately embroidered sky-blue cowboy shirt, replete with fancy, curved breast pockets and powder-pearl snaps instead of buttons. The man was fighting a seemingly losing battle with hair loss, but his eyes were twinkling like a department store Santa Claus on a coffee break and Frost instantly took a liking to the round-faced man.

Monica introduced the doctor as Frost stood and extended his hand.

"Howdy," Frost smiled.

"Howdy, stranger," Titchen drawled slowly in return, the authenticity of his accent riding somewhere between London and Houston, Frost decided. "What brings you to these here parts?"

Frost mentally and physically shrugged—he'd play the cowboy game. "That's what I aim to find out, Doc."

Monica offered to get them each a bottle of Watney's, but the doctor wouldn't hear of it—for himself or for Frost.

"Another time, thank you, ma'am." Monica's Piccadilly cowboy signaled to Frost to take a seat on one of the bar stools. "Monica tells me you can't remember much about your past, young fella."

"Not a thing, Doc."

"Hmmm." Titchen rummaged around in his black bag until he produced a penlight, which he turned on and shined directly into Frost's eye. "Hmmm. Hmmm." The doctor moved the penlight, Frost feeling Titchen explore his scalp with the finger tips of his right hand. "Ah ha."

"Find something?" Frost questioned, not liking at all the tone of the doctor's ah ha. He felt his hair being parted by the M.D.'s fingers.

"Yep, young fella—reckon I did. It seems you've recently suffered a severe blow to the head. Do you, by chance, recall being bushwhacked?"

"No, can't say that I do," Frost laughed, in spite of himself. "If I did get hit on the head—would that explain my memory loss?"

Titchen answered in the affirmative, "Yes, your Hollywood screenwriters notwithstanding, a severe blow to the head can, most assuredly, give way to amnesia." Titchen cleared his throat. "You have a slight horizontal laceration, approximately two-and-one-half inches in diameter, just above the right ear, and unless I'm mistaken, the markings of the wound would seem to indicate that a bullet creased your skull. If that is the case—you're one very fortunate hombre."

Frost swiveled the stool around to face the doctor.

"There's no present danger, of course," Titchen continued, "other than that someone apparently tried to dry gulch you and failed, so may be looking to try for you again." Titchen stood, clicked off the penlight and placed it back in his black bag. "I do note signs of a possible concussion, but can't make any sound conclusions without examining X-rays of your skull. I suggest you not have anything more to drink tonight, get a good eight hour's shut-eye, then mosey on over and see me in the morning. Monica knows the way and can bring you in her buckboard. All right, then?"

"Thanks, Doc."

"Good." Titchen closed his black bag and then tilted his head in Monica's direction, speaking in his cockney-Texas drawl, "Evening, ma'am." He nodded over to Frost. "Son. If you all will excuse me, I'm a-gonna head on home to the ranch."

"And polish your spurs?" Frost suggested.

"Heck, no—rustle up some grub then get me a glass of redeye." He let Monica help him on with his raincoat, then waved farewell from the door. "Adios."

Frost waved back. "You forgot to leave me a silver bullet," he said hopefully.

Chapter Four

The door to his room burst open and Frost reacted automatically—the Browning High Power was in his right hand, the muzzle of the 9mm aimed at the sound.

"Hey!" Monica Hewlett-Jones gasped, standing frozen within the framework of the doorway, a breakfast tray laden with food clutched in her shaking hands. "You don't mess around!"

"Sorry," Frost apologized, sitting up in bed, arranging two pillows to support his back—and feeling rather silly as he lowered the Browning. "Talk about biting the hand that feeds you, huh?"

"Damn right," she smiled, entering the room and setting the tray on the bed so it rode over Frost's lap. "You'd have to find somebody else to cook you breakfast. Pulling the gun on me like that tells us something important, though—your response wasn't something conscious. Whatever you do nine-to-five when your memory's going one hundred percent, your success or failure seems to depend on your reaction time. Maybe you're a syndicate killer or something," she concluded brightly.

"Great. So now we know I use a Zippo lighter and react instantly to danger. The thick plottens, like they say." He glanced down at the scrambled eggs, bacon, sausage, and a round, toasted bun scored with dozens of holes and filled with butter. A cup with strawberry jam in it was off to the side. "Don't tell me," Frost said, picking up the butter-covered bun, "it's an English muffin—right?"

"Wrong," Monica corrected. "That's what's known as a crumpet."

"That's odd. I always thought a crumpet was the same thing as a tart."

"Which tells us something more about your past," she laughed.

"What's that?" Frost asked.

"You didn't make your money as a stand-up comedian."

"Ha ha," the one-eyed man chuckled. "But seriously—the breakfast looks great. Do you mind if I . . . ?"

"Of course not. Eat up before it gets cold."

"Thanks," Frost said, grabbing for a rasher of crispy bacon and finding it saltier than he expected. "Delicious." There was a small pot of tea next to his plate and he poured himself a cup. "It seems late. How long was I out?"

"Long enough to get more than twelve hours of sleep," Monica told him. "And also long enough for me to pop down to Marks & Spencers and buy you some new clothes."

"Thanks again. What'd ya use to size them with—the rags I had on last night?"

"That's right. And then I threw them away. But I took

37

all the labels out just in case we need them to establish your identity—I read about doing that in a novel once. I'll bring up what I bought you after breakfast." She turned to leave, then stopped herself. "There's a small shelf underneath the tray. When you've finished eating, you'll find this morning's paper. I'll be back up later to check on you."

Frost told the woman thanks—again—and watched as she left the room, then worked his way through the eggs, bacon, sausage and crumpet. After pouring himself a second cup of tea, he lifted the breakfast tray from his lap and set it to the side; finding room for the tray was no problem because the bed in Monica's guest room was a king-size. Frost took a sip of the tea, then reached beneath the tray for the newspaper—the morning edition of *The Guardian*.

The headlines told of negotiations underway to avert an impending national railway strike, but it was a photograph, prominently displayed in the lower right-hand corner of page one, that captured his immediate attention—and caused the back of his head to suddenly start to ache badly.

The picture was of a woman—blonde and pretty—whose face was somehow familiar to him. A news story entitled, *"Journalist Disappears"* accompanied the photo and, somehow unable to resist, the one-eyed man felt compelled to read the account of the woman's disappearance,

The woman's name was Bess Stallman, and the sight of the name in print made Frost's head ache even more. She was a journalist with I.N.B.—International News Bureau—and had been recalled from her American post to fill her former position with the London-based news agency when her replacement with I.N.B. had died under what the local authorities were calling mysterious circumstances.

Last seen in the company of her fiance, a professional soldier named Henry Frost, and a Mr. Michael O'Hara, occupation unlisted, Miss Stallman had been missing for more than forty-eight hours. Since that time her superiors at I.N.B. had been unsuccessful in their attempts to locate Miss Stallman or the two men she was supposed to have been with. When questioned regarding the case, the detective assigned to the investigation would only state that foul play was not suspected at this time. Further developments in the case would be made public as soon as they became available.

With the back of his skull feeling like a dozen freight trains were playing demolition derby inside his head, Frost folded the paper and dropped it to his lap, leaning against the pillows, closing his eye, urging himself to drive the burning pain from his mind before it consumed him. But it was no good.

Each time he thought he might be winning the war against the series of explosions going off in his head, scattered images he either wanted to forget or else couldn't recognize would leap to the center of his mind, and all the hurt he was experiencing would come flooding back, stronger than ever.

The room grew warm to him. He was roasting suddenly, sweat dripping from his armpits, his legs, his hands. His vision was blurred and his tongue felt like too many cigarettes. He kicked the quilted covers from his body, sending his half-empty cup of tea tumbling from the breakfast tray and onto the bed.

He swung his legs off the bed, lowering his feet to the

floor, the walls of the room swimming before his eye. He wiped the back of his hand across his forehead and the knuckles came away dripping, sopping wet with sweat.

"I'm burning up," Frost muttered to himself. His breaths were coming in short, ragged huffs. He was trapped in the middle of a fire and he had to put the fire out. And there was only one place he knew to do that.

Pushing himself away from the bed, Frost stood— sweat clinging the material of the pajama bottoms to him like a second skin. His knees were shaking and he felt waves of nausea as he crossed to the bedroom doorway, his breathing even rougher now, his hands, bracing against the door frame, all that was keeping him erect.

More bombs detonated in his head as he reached for the doorknob, groping for it, turning it with his slippery fingers once it was found. Then he was in the hallway— half walking, half stumbling while he covered the short distance from the bedroom to the bathroom.

Almost falling through the door, Frost tore off his pajama bottoms and stepped into the shower stall, his hands working the faucets, running the water, one finger punching out to depress the lever activating the shower head—the water spurting, cold at first, then warm, but still so very much cooler than the flames eating him inside.

And the water splashed then upon the blue tiles of the shower stall, drenching his body, raining down on him, bright colors taking shape in his mind—forming, solidifying, becoming all too real.

The shapes were armed men, dangerous men, perhaps in the military, coming for him, chasing him, running him down like an animal caught in a hunt, backing him to the edge of a cliff, high above a bottomless pit. Gunfire then—fast and fierce—Frost was screaming, feeling the pain, backing away and then falling, sinking down forever into the bottomless pit of no return. Sinking down, down, down. . . .

Frost opened his eye and realized he was sitting on his bare rear end on the floor of the shower stall, the spray from the shower head driving into his body like icy cold needles, the supply of hot water long since used up he knew. His hands were shaking and so was the rest of his body as he attempted to stand, the strength of his quivering knees giving out before he'd raised himself six inches.

It was shivering cold inside his body. His teeth were clicking together uncontrollably and he thought he might have bitten his tongue. He spit and the icy water between his legs went pink for a second before the blood washed down the drain. He closed his eye, too weak to reach up and turn the faucets off. The burning had ended and the fires were out, but he wasn't feeling any better now that—

Someone hit the shower off and Frost looked up. It was Monica—kicking off her shoes, stepping into the stall, scooping her hands around his chest and under his arms, lifting him, pulling him up, cooing to him to get to his feet, telling him not to worry and that everything was going to be all right, telling him to listen to her and to help her help him stand.

And the one-eyed man did listen.

Frost felt himself rising, standing in the shower, his mind clearing to the reality of his surroundings, Monica encircling his body with her arms, supporting his weight, preventing him from falling down again.

"Are you . . . are you OK?" she asked, the fabric of her blouse made transparent as her breasts pushed against the wetness of his body. "Are you?"

"I'm cold," was all Frost got out, one part of his mind threatening to black out, another vaguely aware of how Monica's nipples were hardening against his chest. "Freezing."

Monica held him tighter and Frost moved forward, stepping from the shower stall, dripping his way across the floor, one foot after another, Monica leading him from the bathroom to the hall and into a big, comfortable bed—hers not his. The feel of velour then as a soft, plush towel dried his body. "Better," he said, his teeth chattering still. "Cold, though."

Her hands eased him down onto the bed, the covers turned back, the sensation of the sheets welcoming against his skin, the woman's fingers grasping his ankles, pulling his legs up and off the floor, sliding them beneath the quilted bedspread.

"I'll be right back," she promised.

And in a moment—it could have been an hour—she was.

His arms and legs were beginning to thaw as he watched Monica, standing beside the bed, popping open the buttons of her blouse, shrugging it from her shoulders, exposing her breasts, high and firm, her nipples—the flesh taut and coppery pink. Hooking her thumbs under the waistband of her skirt, she pushed her hands down, taking the skirt with her. She was no girl—a grown woman instead, her hips rounded, her legs long and beautiful. She kicked free of the skirt. Only her panties remained—lavender colored and not much of them. She sat on the bed, pushing them down as she did, stepping out of the panties with her left leg, the ankle of her right hooking them. Her right leg snapped out and up

42

and the panties too were gone.

He was already becoming erect as Monica slipped into bed next to him, pulling the covers over them both, pressing her body against him, her breasts against his chest, covering his body with hers, warming him.

"Monica," he whispered. "This wasn't—wasn't a con."

"I don't care if it was," she whispered, her breath against his face.

She held him in her arms, rolling to the left, taking him with her, until she was on her back and Frost on top of her. As he moved between her thighs, she whispered again, "I don't care if it was."

Frost wondered what had happened to the cold.

Chapter Five

"Who is he?"

"Who?"

"The guy on the other side of the room." Frost pointed him out. "The one talking to the woman with the beehive on her head."

"It's a wig," Monica laughed.

"That's her problem," Frost said. "Do you know the guy she's talking to?"

Monica nodded. "Of course—he's Sir John Pinkham-Fletcher. He's with the British Foreign Service. Why do you ask—do you recognize him?"

"It's not that," confessed the one-eyed man, sipping at his vodka and orange juice. "Several times during the evening I've caught him looking at me."

"Maybe he fancies you?"

"You think so?"

"From what I've heard, he might. Some men are all too dramatic and obvious when they try to play musical beds and all that. Seeing as how you are the only one-eyed man at the party, it could also be that Sir John is just rudely curious. Hmmm?"

"Maybe," Frost murmured.

It was a dinner party in Kensington—one of those wear-a-smile-and-try-to-be-pleasant-all-night-long kind of get togethers that Frost instinctively knew he hated. Under any other circumstances he would have refused to attend, but because Monica had insisted a night out would do him some good, he had relented. Originally, the plan of attack called for him to escort Monica to the party. Once there he was supposed to mix and mingle with the forty or so guests in attendance, Monica's theory being that doing so might serve to help jog his memory into place—anyone who was anyone in London would drop in, she had advised him.

Looking back, Frost had to admit the idea did have its merits. Pieces of his fleeting memory had been trickling in since he'd first opened his eye in the rain-swept alley the day before. Going on that basis, it made sense, seemed logical, that getting out in a crowd could be the best thing for him to do. But now, more than three hours after arriving for the dinner party, Frost was ready to give it up as a bad idea. Monica's plan for triggering his memory back into line was so far a total failure.

Sir John Pinkham-Fletcher openly watched him during the course of the evening. Wearing an eye patch made him conspicuous in any crowd. For all Frost knew, many of the others attending the dinner party had been staring too, but were more adept than Sir John in concealing their curiosity.

Frost finished his drink, his second since dinner, and set the cocktail glass on the cork-topped coaster on the bar to his left. Out of the corner of his eye he was aware that Sir John had seized the opportunity to look at him again, but when Frost turned away from the bar, the man Monica had identified as being with the British Foreign Service had hurriedly resumed his conversation with the woman wearing the haystack-shaped wig.

From Frost's vantage point Sir John appeared to be in his late forties to early fifties. Well preserved. Of average build, not too heavy or lean, the man was a comfortable compromise somewhere in the middle. With jet black hair—only his hairdresser knows for sure, Frost decided—a distinguished dash of gray showed at the sides, the hair worn in a style which demanded each and every follicle remain in its place or else. Sir John, too, might have been wearing a hairpiece.

"He's been looking at you again," Monica cautioned.

"I know." Frost watched as Sir John leaned in closer to his lady friend, whispering something in her ear that apparently made her laugh, then abruptly turned and was swallowed by the crowd. "So much for that." He smiled at Monica, barely stifling a yawn. "How's our agenda read?"

"Getting bored?"

"Let me put it this way—I'm getting bored."

Monica frowned. "That bad, huh?"

"Yeah. It wouldn't be like we pulled an eat-and-run routine or anything—hmmm? They probably wouldn't even miss us," Frost concluded hopefully. Monica handed him her empty glass and he set it on the bar next to his. "What do ya say we make like a couple of bananas?"

"And split?"

"You got it, kid."

"I say let's say goodbye."

Outside the terraced home in Kensington where the

party inside was still going full swing, Frost and Monica made their way to her Rover, the car parked half a block up the street. The night was cold and damp, the air thick with the promise of rain, and the sky overhead blanketed with a solid wall of clouds reflecting the yellow glow of London's city lights.

A chill wind hit Frost like a slap in the face, reminding him all too well that if Monica's generosity hadn't included a new set of clothes, he would still be freezing his bones away in the torn and tattered rags he'd had on the previous day. As it was, wearing a down-filled bomber jacket, navy blue trousers, long-sleeved blue cotton shirt, and matching lamb's wool sweater, Frost couldn't have been much warmer sitting back at Monica's in front of the fireplace.

"Would you mind driving?" Monica asked when they came to the car. "I had a bit too much to drink at the party and it's not too far to my flat."

Frost raised an eyebrow. "Flat?"

"You know—my apartment in Chelsea," she translated. "Normally, I wouldn't mind taking us home, but the last thing I want is to be stopped by the police for driving under the influence. In England they throw the book at you. They're merciless. How about it?"

"All right—you convinced me." Frost took the keys from her and unlocked the front passenger door for her to get in. "You just steer me in the direction of your place and I'll do the rest." He slammed the door closed, then walked around to the driver's side of the Rover, finding that Monica had already unlocked the door. He got in behind the wheel, pulling the door shut, then inserted the key in the ignition. "How long did it take for you to get used to driving on the left side of the road?"

"Not nervous are you?"

"Me? You gotta be kidding—of course I am." He nudged the clutch to the floorboard and turned the key, gently depressing his other foot on the accelerator, feeling the engine purr to life. "Fantastic," he commented, turning on the headlights. "You hardly hear her running."

"She's a beauty, all right. Cigarette?"

"Thanks—yeah. So, where do we go from here?"

"We're on Eaton Place," Monica said, sounding— Frost thought—like a tour guide, opening her purse, taking her gold cigarette case and removing two of the Dunhill's menthols. She held one in her mouth, snapped her lighter up and lit it, then passed the cigarette over to Frost.

"I can taste your lipstick," he told her quietly.

"How's it taste?"

"Like it did most of the time we were in bed together today." He inhaled, holding the mentholated smoke in his lungs, then slowly exhaling. "It's pretty much the same."

"Is that good or bad?" Monica wanted to know, a teasing sound Frost found interesting coming to her voice.

"Oh, it's good." He reached his left hand out and brought it to rest on her thigh.

Her hand covered his, holding it in place. "Would you like another taste?" Frost looked at her. "Now, as I was saying—we're on Eaton Place right now. To get back to Chelsea and my home all we have to do is go straight ahead and turn to the left. That will give us King's Road, which we'll be able to follow most of the way back."

"Sounds simple enough," he agreed, reluctantly

48

removing his hand from her thigh, taking his foot off the brake, dropping the transmission into first gear, then easing back on the clutch while giving the car some gas.

Frost checked over his shoulder, saw that it was clear, and pulled onto the left-side lane of the street, making for King's Road, the one-eyed man noting that the lavishly expensive homes along Eaton Place were much like Monica's, so far as their outward appearance went, only on a larger scale.

Now that he was back in the Rover, Frost felt more able to relax—something he hadn't been capable of doing while stuck doing time at the party. Although he had taken the precaution of bringing the Browning High Power with them, Monica had convinced him—against his better judgment—to leave the 9mm tucked away in the Rover's glove compartment while they were inside, her reasoning being that, since they weren't sure for certain whether or not Frost knew how to use the gun, carrying the Browning could wind up being a terrible mistake they would later regret.

Fortunately, Frost reflected, his lapse in common sense had not proven disastrous. The gun had not been needed. From now on, though, he told himself, he would play the game using the same rules those who had attempted to kill him had resorted to. And that meant that from now on the Browning High Power would always be with him.

Frost shifted gears and glanced sideways to Monica, her beautiful auburn-colored hair falling over the car seat in a silky cascade. He was tempted to reach out and stroke her hair. He told himself to wait until they were home.

Frost caught a green light at King's Road, signaled with

the Rover's turn indicator, and took a left—moving past an assortment of boutiques and fancy shops, all of them shut down for the night.

"How long to Chelsea?"

"Just a few minutes."

"Good. Just make sure you tell me where to turn—I don't want to have us turn up in Toledo. Holy—!"

"What's wrong?" Monica asked. "Is something the matter?"

Frost increased the pressure of his foot on the gas pedal, sending the Rover surging forward, his eye cautiously alternating its attention from the roadway ahead to what could be seen in the Rover's rear-view mirror. "Unless you're real close friends with the bunch in the two cars behind us, then, yeah—something's the matter. They picked us up right after we hit King's Road."

"Who do you think they are?"

"Not the local Welcome Wagon," he answered sourly. "We gotta try ditching 'em. If I let you out, they might put the bag on you to work against me."

"You're the one driving."

Monica squeezed his hand.

Without warning Frost cut the Rover's wheel in a sharp turn to the right, stomping on the brakes, mashing the clutch to the floor, downshifting, feeling the rear of the Rover fishtailing before straightening out, then he punched the accelerator with his foot, eased off, working the clutch, upshifting into second. The Rover picked up speed, rocketing along—Frost spotted a sign—a narrow avenue called Sydney Street. He hit the clutch again, cut back on the gas, popped the stick into third, then let out the clutch and went back to lead-footing the accelerator.

Tires screeching and engines roaring, the two autos chasing behind them completed the same maneuver—they were following.

"Wonderful," the one-eyed man complained, the half-smoked Dunhill's menthol hanging from the corner of his mouth, a natural extension of his lower lip. "I knew we shoulda stayed at the dinner party. I was having all that fun, but no—you had to—"

"Wha—?" Monica started to protest.

"I'm just wondering if I'll know what the hell to do if those clowns in back catch up to us."

"That's a real confidence-building attitude," Monica told him dryly, glancing over her right shoulder. "Looks like they're gaining on us."

"Enough with the good news," Frost protested, nodding his forehead forward. "What street are we coming to?"

"Fulham Road—Chelsea's to the left."

"Damn!" Frost swore, tapping the brakes, pumping the clutch and downshifting into second, cutting the wheel hard to the right, then back to the left again—marginally steering the Rover around the tail-end of a Volkswagen van backing out onto the street. There was a crashing noise and a fast glance in the rear-view mirror showed him the lead chase car impacting into the van, bouncing away from it, then zooming ahead, its left front headlight smashed and out.

"So much for buying us time," he mumbled, then practically shouted to Monica, "You said Chelsea's to the left?"

"And Hyde Park's to the right."

"It's too dangerous for us to go back to your place. They could have people waiting there for us."

"You're right. So, we'll head for Hyde Park."

"Hyde Park it is," Frost announced at the top of his voice. "Hang on!"

The stop light at Fulham Road—he checked the signal—had just gone red when Frost sent the Rover shooting into the intersection, weaving in and out of the cars that had already started to go with the green. Once the Rover cleared the traffic moving to his left, he kicked his foot down on the brake pedal, working the clutch, downshifting, simultaneously spinning the wheel all the way to the right—throwing the Rover into a slide onto Fulham Road in the direction they wanted to go.

"Sure hope the cops didn't catch me on that one," Frost barked through his gritted teeth, shifting into high gear. "I'm driving without a license!"

Chapter Six

They were running red lights with increasing regularity, having managed to hit only one green out of the last six lights, Frost dodging the opposing traffic cutting across the Rover's path with all the innate talent fear imparts. Twice he'd been convinced the chase was over; once when a stereotypical London taxi cab had nearly come crashing into his side of the Rover—they'd missed colliding by inches. The second close brush with destruction came when one of the city's red double-decker buses cut directly across them. Unable to go around the bus to the left or right, Frost had ridden the Rover's horn while flashing the car's bright lights rapidly on and off, the one-eyed man praying that the bus driver would see him coming and somehow move the bus in time.

Frost had been less than sixty yards away and closing fast when the double decker's driver must have spotted the Rover. Immediately, the bus jerked forward, moving ahead, clearing the intersection as the Rover shot through—the side of Monica's vintage auto scraping against the back end of the bus, shearing off door handles from the sound of it, sending up sparks in the night as metal grated against metal.

But the Rover was free now, racing along Fulham Road, veering in a curve to the left as the street became Brompton Road, Monica told him, small shops and terraced homes whizzing past them in a blur, all the while Frost speeding on a direct course for Hyde Park. What he'd do when he got there, though, he didn't know.

Frost flicked his eye down and to the right to the mirror at the side of the car. "Shit—those guys are still behind us!"

"We haven't lost them?"

"Naw," Frost snarled through his teeth. "Sorry about scrapin' the car up."

"Don't be—it's insured."

"I probably am, too," Frost felt obliged to point out, "but that doesn't make me feel any better. Gone is gone. How about Hyde Park?"

"Dead ahead."

"Love your choice of words." He swerved around to the right, passing a slower-traveling, three-wheeled automobile to his left, cutting back in front of the vehicle the second there was room, almost running the three-wheeler off the road. "That'll teach him to drive the speed limit." Frost goosed the accelerator with the top of his right foot, pushing the Rover's engine to go even faster as they approached the last main intersection before Hyde Park.

"This'll be Knightsbridge," Monica shouted over the engine noise, the street congested. "We'll be in the park once we get to the other side."

"If we get to the other side, you mean," Frost

54

remarked. "Where'd all the cars come from?"

"We're in one of the largest cities in the world—there's bound to be a few."

"Yeah, but it looks like they've all picked tonight, here and now, to come cruise Knightsbridge. Whatever happened to courtesy and consideration?" He checked the picture in the rear-view mirror and concluded it was pretty dismal, looking up in time to see the lead chase car—the one with the smashed-out headlight—as it came plowing into the Rover's rear bumper.

A noise like a thunderclap filled the Rover's interior, the force generated by the impact rocking the car from side to side, Frost fighting desperately to maintain control. The Rover was struck again, throwing it to the left, hopping a curb, then dropping roughly back down to the street, Frost keeping his eye on the intersection at Knightsbridge less than a quarter mile away. "So much for the alignment," he joked, searching for an opening to take them through the snarl of congestion they were racing to meet.

The back of the Rover took another hit to its bumper. Another. Another.

The Rover was shaking on its shocks.

Another hit.

"Damn it—if we don't have a hole to squeeze through when we hit Knightsbridge, those jokers behind us'll bump us into a head-on collision with some of the cross traffic."

Frost saw the stop light at Knightsbridge go from red to green, a minor miracle, he thought. Then a space opened up large enough for him to ease the Rover through. The miracles were adding up fast. The Rover hit the intersection, Frost gunning the last spurt of speed out of the car's engine, cross traffic on Knightsbridge flying by in a blur, the one-eyed man holding his breath as the Rover rode into and out of a dip in the road, the entire car seeming to leave the ground, the wheels touching down again. Frost let out his breath, and then it was all over—the busy intersection of Knightsbridge and Brompton Road was behind them and they were tearing down a small expanse of roadway, rushing by an area Monica designated as Edinburgh Gate, and pulling onto the woods and water acreage of Hyde Park.

"Made it," Frost said, breathing deeply. "How about our . . . ?"

"Still behind us," Monica shouted. "We didn't lose them. They cut across the intersection the same time we did."

"The night's still young!" Frost clenched the burnt filter tip of the Dunhill's between his teeth, braking the car, downshifting, cutting the wheels in a rubber-peeling turn to the left, losing traction, fighting the steering wheel spinning in his hands. Regaining traction, Frost felt the tires take hold as he worked the clutch, shifting up into second, then third, his right foot pressing down hard on the accelerator.

They were speeding along a road less than fifty feet wide—clearly one designed for something besides an improvised race track. From what Frost could tell the park was deserted. Off to his left there were a few street lights, but to his right, inside the body of the park itself, he could see nothing but dim shapes and outlines in the foggy blackness.

The tiny road made a sweeping curve to the right and as Frost headed the Rover into it he watched over his shoulder as the second car chasing them left the road and began moving across the park grounds—intending to cut the Rover off, Frost realized, when the road widened coming out of the curve. He guessed the road doubled back in the direction of where they had first entered the park.

"We need another miracle," Frost decided, bringing the Rover out of the curve, shifting into high gear, checking in the rear-view to see that the lead chase car was less than a hundred feet behind them. Up ahead and closing fast was the second chase car, riding the bumps and paths of the park, trying to intercept the Rover before it could get by. A sickly chill creeping up Frost's spine told him that chase car number two would have no trouble cutting them off.

"They're trying to sandwich us in," Monica stated the obvious.

"No shit."

Frost shut up and stared hard as the headlights of the second car abruptly quit moving, the car less than twenty yards from the road. Ten seconds later they passed it, Frost laughing out loud at the sight of the chase car that had been making tracks to head them off—buried up to its hubcaps in what looked like a giant mud puddle. Frost saw the doors to the stuck car burst open as four beefy-looking men piled out, and he couldn't resist the temptation—he beeped his horn and waved to the men as the Rover flew by them. The next instant, the side-view mirror disintegrated in a flurry of metal and glass.

"Jeez!" Frost snapped, crunching himself down into the seat, his left hand flashing out, forcing Monica down. "They're shooting at us!"

"I didn't hear anything," Monica admitted.

"Neither did I, but that's what they're doing. Keep

your head low and out of sight. They're gonna fire again."

And as if in response to his prediction, three loud pings, coming together so fast that they almost sounded like one, slapped against the Rover's rear, making a trio of spider-webbing holes in the windshield in front of him.

Involuntarily, Frost felt himself sinking lower into his seat.

"Another inch and you'll be sitting on the floor." Monica shifted in her seat, keeping her head down like Frost. "How much of the road can you see?"

"What road?"

"That's what I thought. Maybe now would be a good time to get that gun of yours out of the glove box?"

"Can you get it without giving them a target?"

"I can get it—but then what?"

"Get it and then we'll see. Huh?"

"All right." The woman riding beside Frost turned around in her seat, reaching out to the glove compartment, pulling it open, removing the Browning High Power from inside. "Got it."

"Good. Hang onto it. We got a turn coming up—a real good one."

Running through the braking-downshifting-turning-the-car-around routine that was becoming automatic for him now, Frost put the Rover through a zigzagging turn, back and to the left. He fed the engine more gas and began shifting into higher gears once out of the turn, checking out what he could see of the park terrain to his right.

"Is that what I think it is over there—a lagoon?" he asked.

"Yes, the Serpentine. It's a small lake."

"We lost one car to the mud. Maybe we can get the

guys in back there to go for a swim."

"How?"

"Details, details," Frost protested. "I'll think of something."

But there wasn't the chance. Bullets shattered whole chunks out of the windshield, the car lurching as there was an exploding sound—the right front tire was gone. Frost tried to keep the Rover under control.

The shooting stopped, the Rover spinning out. Frost was losing it. He sat bolt upright in his seat, both hands fighting the steering wheel, battling to prevent the Rover from smashing into the side of a small building rushing up to them, the sudden realization that his efforts to avoid the building were useless.

"Hit the floor—cover your head!" he shouted, then the front end of the Rover was skidding off the road, shuddering to a halt against the side of the building. The force of the crash threw Frost forward, his forehead striking the steering wheel, red and green floaters washing across his eye. Dazed, the one-eyed man fought to stay conscious, a vague portion of his mind shouting to him that the car was on fire.

"Shit," Frost grumbled, annoyed partly because he couldn't pass out, wiping blood away from a cut on his head and grabbing for Monica. "You OK?"

"Smoke?" the woman coughed. "We're burning!"

"You got my gun?"

"Here." She slapped the weapon into his hand, then Frost popped open the door on his side of the car and leaped out—keeping hold of Monica and pulling her out with his left hand, gripping the High Power in his right fist like it was—somehow—a normal extension of his hand.

He crouched low, Monica beside him, hugging the wall of the building they had hit, while flames enveloped the Rover in a blinding whoosh of heat and yellow fire. They had seconds left before the gas tank exploded. Automatic weapons fired at their heels as Frost ran to get around the corner of the wall, shoving Monica ahead of him, pushing her around the side of the building and diving for cover himself as the Rover's gas tank blew.

The fireball belched skyward making the night blacker in contrast—shards of the blown-apart Rover showering everywhere, a bright orange-and-black ball of flame and smoke engulfing the once-pristine car.

"That . . . that could have been us," gasped Monica.

"Still could be," Frost advised, looking around the edge of the building. The car that had been chasing them had been abandoned on the road about a hundred feet from their position. The gunmen from inside it were nowhere to be seen. "What's the building we hit?"

"Where the people who come to swim change into their bathing suits."

"In this weather? They'd have to be penguins." He ran the back of his hand across the cut on his forehead.

"You're bleeding."

"Bashed my head on the steering wheel," Frost explained. "Wasn't wearing my seat belt."

"It didn't jog your memory back—getting hit on the head? Like you see in the movies?"

"I wish, but no—all I got is one helluva headache. Something better happen and soon, I'll tell ya that much. If all these people are going to be tryin' to bump me off, then I want to know the reason why. Hold on."

With Monica as safe as possible behind the wall of the building, Frost crept forward, trying to pinpoint where the men from the car were hiding, getting his head around the corner for less than five seconds before a ragged burst of slugs slapped into the wall above his face. Frost drew back and out of range before he had a chance to see where the shots had been fired from.

There were scattered clumps of trees on the opposite side of the street, across from the changing rooms and the still burning and crackling wreck of the Rover, any one of the trees wide enough in their trunks to partially conceal the gunners. With the obviously silencer-equipped weapons they were using, zeroing in on where they were shooting from was all but impossible. The one-eyed man's head ached for an instant—why did he know they had to be using silencers?

Thumbing off the safety on the cocked and locked Browning High Power, Frost turned and doubled back— the building housing the changing rooms to his left, the small lake inside Hyde Park off to his immediate right, getting most of the way to where Monica was waiting when a shadowy man-shape came charging around the corner of the building behind her, the SMG clamped in an assault position in the man's hands impossible to miss.

The weapon was coming on line, up and around to Monica. She fell to her knees. Frost fired a two-round, semi-automatic burst from the Browning, striking the gunman dead on his feet. The body twitched in a toppling slide to the left, then fell like a limp rag, tumbling from the tiny platform in back of the building, splashing head-first into the lake.

Frost made a grab for the bottom of the dead man's trouser leg, but the body was sinking quickly, taking it and the SMG the killer's dead fingers still gripped beyond Frost's reach. The one-eyed man's hand was just leaving the water when a sound from off to his left made him wheel. Another man, this one wielding a blade the size of a machete, was coming to cut Frost down.

With the blade held high, already starting the down swing, the one-eyed man pumped the Browning's trigger once, then once more; the body, quivering with the twin impacts, fell. Frost approached the man, a fast kick with the toe of his right shoe to the man's left temple finishing him.

"No sense being messy," Frost rasped to Monica—still on her knees—the one-eyed man already dragging the body toward the platform over the small lake. A quick frisk—no gun—and Frost rolled the body in. There had been no wallet either, no identification.

"You just shot him," Monica said, back on her feet and standing next to Frost. "You just shot him like you did the first one."

"There can't really be that many creatively different ways to shoot a guy—somehow I just know that," Frost told her, aware once again that his instincts had saved him. Whenever he needed to call on his abilities they were there, waiting to be tapped, with no second-guessing or confusion to get in his way.

"Where'd you learn . . . learn to, ahh, to do that?" the woman asked.

"That's what I'd like to know, too," Frost laughed quietly. "Come on." Cautiously hurrying from the platform dock area behind the building alongside the lake, Frost led Monica in the direction of where the two men had parked their car. If the engine could be hot wired or—miracle of miracles—the key was still in the ignition, Frost knew the car would be their fastest ticket out of Hyde Park. They were halfway home when squealing tires and headlights dancing across the night told the one-eyed man that the second car chasing them was no longer trapped in the mud.

Mentally, Frost calculated that even if they got to the parked car and the keys were in the ignition, the second chase car would be on them before he would have time to get the engine going.

Monica held him tightly by the arm. "What do we do now?"

"Run," Frost answered. And they ran.

Chapter Seven

"All we got to be is stuck in the middle of the bridge when those suckers pull up for a chat and they got us," Frost told her, leaving the road which led to the bridge going over the Serpentine. "We get trapped out there and there's no place for us to run. They wouldn't even have to shoot us. They could just run us down."

"OK, I'm a believer," Monica told him, not matching Frost's long stride step for step, but half-jogging to keep up. "We don't have to take the bridge. If you say no, then I say no."

"Good," Frost told her, smiling in spite of himself, holding her right hand in his left, his right hand with a death grip on the Browning.

They were entering a small wooded area moments later, an area Monica had identified as Kensington Gardens, immediately next to Hyde Park. The mud-covered car pursuing them roared from the path along the Serpentine and onto the road leading to the bridge, screeching to a halt, its occupants out and apparently debating which direction to continue their search.

Seeing the car alone told Frost that, in all probability, the car belonging to the pair of dead men back at the lake's changing rooms hadn't had a key in its ignition; otherwise it would be in use now as well. He was pleased with himself because it meant his intuitive senses were acting equally as strong as his physical and combative instincts were.

The next bunch of trees was thirty feet away as they began running for them, leaving the path they had been using, improvising one of their own, reaching the protection of the trees moments before the chase car's engine started to race—away from the bridge and straight for the trees where Frost and Monica were hiding.

"Shit," Frost swore wearily. He tugged on Monica's hand and ran deeper into the gardens, the one-eyed man deliberately picking his way along the muddiest trail he could find, seeking great slippery patches of the stuff, counting on the fact that, having already been buried in the mud once that night, the killers would probably go out of their way to avoid getting stuck again.

And he was right. At the first unsuitably muddy patch of ground the killers came to, the driver of the pursuit car stopped and everybody piled out. Keeping to the obscure protection of a single tree, Frost hugged the ground, watching, shielding Monica's body with his own. The man who had been riding shotgun moved in front of the car, silhouetting himself against the running lights. Frost didn't shoot—the risk was too high. The gunman opened fire with the silenced SMG he carried—sweeping the weapon back and forth, hosing the target area. He wanted them to break and run. Frost smiled.

With the dull, coughing sputter of the SMG barely audible, Frost kept his arms surrounding Monica as the mud near to them exploded, but none of the slugs came close to the tree behind which they were hiding.

"What now?" Monica whispered, feeling to Frost like she had taken root to the ground. "What are we going to—?"

"Shhh!"

"Awright," the gunman shooting the SMG shouted loudly in a strong British accent, replacing his gun's spent magazine with a fresh one he took from inside his coat. "They're not far off from here—they can't be. So, we got to split up. Harry and me'll take the path by the lake. George go to the left toward the refreshment stand."

"How 'bout me?" a fourth voice asked.

"You, Pete—you go straight in through the trees and over to Lancaster Road."

"Cor!" the voice—Pete—grumbled. "Look at all the blinkin' mud. They ain't gonna be that far."

"I didn't say that they were," the apparent leader of the group shouted back. "I only told you to look that way to be sure."

"But what about 'Arold and Dave first?"

"Sod 'em," the leader barked. "We'll find 'em after we're finished here. Now—move your arse and quit wasting my bloody time. We got work to do. Move it!"

The leader went around to the driver's side of the car and killed the running lights, plunging the gardens into inky darkness, then joined the man Frost guessed was Harry, both men taking up the path along the lake. The one named George set off to Frost's right. It left only Pete—who waited until his three compatriots had all been swallowed by the night before following orders and doing what he was told—cutting across the gardens through the mud. Frost could see it would lead him directly to the tree they were using for cover.

Monica saw that too, but when her body tensed and she started to rise, Frost braced his hands on her shoulders, keeping her in place. His instructions were simple. "Stay here. Don't move." Then he was up on his feet, moving low to the ground, moving in a circle he expected would take him around and in back of his closest foe.

Frost could not rate for certain the professional qualifications of the remaining three men tracking them down, but Pete, sloughing through the mud with the constant sucking noises his feet were making, was easy. The man was a low-life amateur, a little kid playing a big kid's game. Only now the bullets in the guns were real, not pretend, Frost mused.

Frost was almost into position when Pete came even with the tree protecting Monica and stopped in his sticky tracks, wheeling to the left, swinging his SMG around to bear down on the woman.

"Hold it, asshole," Frost advised coldly, digging the muzzle of the Browning into Pete's right ear. "Any bullshit and you're dead meat, boy."

But Pete made his play, twisting on his feet, bringing his hands around with the subgun, Frost cold-cocking him with the Browning halfway through the turn.

Pete's expression of shocked disbelief and pain registered on his face as Frost caught him under the arms and lowered him to the ground.

"Idiot," Frost rasped, rifling through the pockets of the coat Pete was wearing and finding two spare magazines for the SMG Pete had dropped, sliding both of them into his belt under his bomber jacket. He took Pete's belt and shoelaces—the shoelaces wet with mud—and tied the man's hands and feet so it would take an hour or so of hard trying to get himself untied. He left the mouth without a gag—if Pete distracted his friends by shouting for help, it could not hurt. A more detailed search of Pete's pockets produced a multiblade Swiss Army knife, but no I.D.

Satisfied that the odds against them had been lessened, Frost eased the Browning into his belt, the safety upped, and crossed to Pete's orphaned submachine gun, picking it up, noting with not much surprise that the weapon's safety was still on.

Frost hefted the weight of the SMG in his hands, releasing its safety, then wheeling swiftly to his left and opening fire at the onrushing figure of the man named George, George already firing, too.

Bullets thudding into the ground and trees all about him, Frost pumped the subgun's trigger—neat three-round bursts, Frost somehow knowing automatically that the gun he held was a Sten MK II, his fire impacting George, ripping across the man's belly and thighs.

George screamed and died, jackknifing, flipping flat onto his face and into the mud, the Sten he'd been using—identical to Frost's—covered by his body. Frost tensed, hearing the advance of the last two men through the trees. Sensing somehow that the magazine of the Sten MK II was about to run dry, his fingers went through the necessary motions, dropping the spent stick, yanking a fresh one from his belt under his jacket, ramming it home, slapping the baseplate, seating it, then turning to face the two men charging at him.

"Come and get me, suckers!" Frost snarled, anger for the fight in the alley, the auto chase through London, the endangering of Monica—all of it—making him want the men dead. Now.

His finger twitched against the trigger. He could feel mud splattering around him, hear the whistling sounds as the slugs tore through the air around him. He kept pumping the trigger. His magazine was dry. He heard Monica screaming, "Stop it! Stop it! They're dead already—they're dead—whoever the hell you are!"

He turned to look at her—she was sinking to the ground beside a tree trunk, her face ashen in the poor light. "They're dead," she almost whispered to him.

"Yes," he told her quietly. "Yes."

Chapter Eight

Unable to return to Monica's apartment in Chelsea because of the likelihood that it was under surveillance, Frost and the woman decided to do the next best thing— drive down to Monica's cottage estate in Surrey.

Transportation for the ride was the Ford which the second group of killers had been chasing them in. Unlike the pursuit car abandoned near the Serpentine's changing rooms, the mud-covered Ford still had a key in its ignition. Not only that, Frost noted, after stowing the four SMGs he'd confiscated in the Ford's trunk and climbing behind the wheel of the car as soon as Monica was secure in the passenger seat, but the Ford's gas tank was three-quarters full, more than an ample amount to get them to Surrey.

With Monica providing directions, Frost quickly enough had them well away from Hyde Park and Kensington Gardens, leaving London and heading east on the M25 expressway, then south on the M23 for the Surrey countryside. For the balance of the ride, once he had the Ford on a route which demanded little more than keeping the car on the road, Frost drove in silence, Monica quiet, staring into the darkness, the whistle of the slipstream through the partially open driver's side window the only sound above the pulse of the motor.

It was becoming increasingly crucial for him to unlock the secret of his identity, the one-eyed man realized. Since waking in the dirty, rain-swept alley, no less than ten strangers had attempted, albeit unsuccessfully, to kill him. Bad enough on its own. What compounded his concern was that now, because she had come to his aid, Monica was scheduled for the same. The force behind the mysterious series of attacks was looking to put the pair of them permanently out of action. That much at least was obvious. Frost couldn't help believing that Monica would have been way ahead of the game if she'd never helped him at all.

Frost felt emotionally and morally obligated to protect her. When first reaching the Ford, he had earnestly suggested to her that it would be safer for her on all counts if she simply dropped him off at the next corner and took herself to the police for protection. But Monica had simply said, "No."

He judged they'd been on the road for forty-five minutes or so when they turned off, heading up the winding drive to Monica's cottage. There was no moon out, nor were there rows of lights bordering the drive to guide them along, but Frost, glancing left to right on the quarter mile or so stretch of driveway—the Ford's headlights on high beam—could tell that the grounds surrounding the woman's country home were impeccably well cared for.

A miniature forest of trees was bisected by the driveway they were following.

"Looks nice," Frost observed, bringing the Ford out of a curve and around a bend in the drive—directly in front of a massive building two stories high, reaching, Frost estimated, more than two hundred feet from end to end. He nudged the brakes, stopping the car, the headlights of the Ford bathing the building in their glow. "I thought you said we were going to your cottage?"

"We are. This is it."

"Cottage?" Frost murmured, easing his foot off the brake and pulling the rest of the way up the drive, finally coming to a complete halt in front of the cottage's main entrance—a broad double door topped with a half circle of gleaming yellow glass. "I've seen smaller cities."

Monica laughed. "Give the place a chance. You'll like it."

Before they had time to get out of the car, the front doors to the woman's country home were thrown open and a wrinkled old man emerged, bouncily moving down the walk leading to the driveway.

"Madam," the old man spoke, holding out his hand and helping Monica to step from the Ford. "I was not informed that Madam would be joining us this evening. In that event I should have prepared for Madam's arrival."

"No problem, Graham," Monica answered. "My being here tonight has nothing to do with plans I had made in advance. My friend and I," she nodded, indicating Frost, "found ourselves in an unavoidably sticky situation in London, and thought it best if we came down here to get away from it all."

"I understand, Mrs. Hewlett-Jones," the man Monica had addressed as Graham replied, though Frost couldn't see how understanding could be possible.

"Has madam any luggage this evening?" Graham asked, speaking in a slow, almost melodious manner.

"Not this time," Monica informed him. "But there are other, more pressing matters, I would like you to attend to."

"Yes?" Graham stood at attention awaiting his orders. "And what would these pressing matters consist of, madam?"

Monica pointed to the Ford. "I should like this car my friend and I have stolen to be wiped free of fingerprints and then disposed of in a suitable location."

"Yes, madam. And will there be anything else madam requires concerning the automobile?" Graham didn't bat an eye.

"Don't forget the, ah, items stashed in the trunk," Frost suggested.

"Oh, yes. Also, Graham—in the boot of the Ford you will find four submachine guns. Please remove them and bring them safely inside before you dispose of the car. I think that should do it." She looked to Frost for additional necessities.

"That about wraps it up," Frost smiled.

"Yes, Graham, then that should be all. My friend and I will see to our personal needs on our own."

"Very good, madam." Graham bowed slightly, the corners of his wrinkled mouth turning up in a smile. "Then, if you'll excuse me, I shall see about securing the proper materials for the removal of the fingerprints." Frost, Monica taking his arm, started into the house. Graham sounded like a handy man to have around.

"So, how many centuries has Graham been in the family?" Frost inquired, turning down an offer for one of Monica's mentholated Dunhill's in favor of a drink.

73

"As far as I know, Graham came with the house," Monica joked, pouring Frost's drink and holding it out for him to take. "I hope you like it—it's Myers's Rum."

"Myers's?" Frost hesitated, wondering why the name or the rum should be of any significance to him, then shrugged. "That'll be fine—thanks." He accepted the glass and took a drink, swallowing the rum, enjoying the pleasing warmth it provided, frowning unexpectedly as an image flashed through his mind.

Like the flashback he'd experienced while at Monica's apartment, Frost saw himself again facing a group of armed men, the ones who might have been soldiers. As they attacked, the one-eyed man came to realize that his right hand wasn't empty. It was holding a handgun. A particularly large one. He lifted the gun, took aim on the adversary closest to him and fired. There was a thundering, booming noise as his target took a direct hit to the face—the recoil from the tremendous discharge of the oversized handgun hurting Frost's hand.

He closed his eye and shook his head. And when he opened his eye the fleeting image of the large handgun clamped in his right fist was gone, replaced instead by the reality of the glass of Myers's Rum.

"Are you okay?" Frost heard Monica ask.

"Huh? Yeah, I'm fine. Blanked out there for a second, I guess. How'd you know?"

"Your expression—something about it was wrong." She sipped at her own glass of rum. "Another piece of your puzzle?"

Frost nodded. "This piece involving a handgun, but not clear enough for me to make it out."

"Hmmm." Monica pursed her lips. "Guns seem to be playing an important role in your life lately. Bring your

74

drink and come with me," she said—impulsively, Frost thought. She reached over and switched off the light over the bar. "There's something I want you to see."

Monica led and Frost followed, leaving the bar, walking together down a long, carpeted hallway, Frost tasting his drink again—the mental picture of the large handgun booming in his fist, there for a second, then gone once more. Then they were standing in front of an open doorway.

"This was Jonathan's study." Monica turned on a muted overhead light. "You should find it interesting."

They stepped further into the room and Frost's eye twitched. Most definitely, he found the study of Monica's late husband of interest, crossing the room until he was standing before a glass cabinet at least twenty feet wide— a glass cabinet filled with an assortment of guns.

"Quite a collection," Frost stated, beginning at one end of the cabinet and visually working his way down, admiring the weapons on display. "Quite a collection."

"Don't I know it?" the woman agreed. "Jonathan took great pride in owning and collecting them. I understand it's a well-rounded collection."

"No argument there." Frost had slowly inspected a third of the collection. "But I always thought England had strict laws preventing collections like this, though."

"The laws aren't like those in the States—that's for sure, but the legal hassles Jonathan endured to put this collection together were worth it."

"Quick!" Frost suddenly snapped. "A key to the cabinet—do you have one?"

"Sure." She went to a bookcase stacked floor-to-ceiling with volumes of books, one of which she pulled from the shelf. "Since Jonathan liked to refer to his gun collection as the second greatest treasure in his life—I was his first—we decided to hide the key to the cabinet in here, inside the front cover of this leather-bound edition of *Treasure Island*." Monica withdrew the key from its hiding place, set the book on the study's desk, then went to the cabinet and inserted the key into a tiny, gold-colored lock. A twist of her wrist and the doors to the cabinet swung open. "There you go."

Immediately, Frost's hand reached out and into the cabinet, his fingers wrapping around the butt of one of the handguns. "This is it," he murmured. He held the gun for Monica to see, then held it up to the light for a closer inspection. "It's a .44 Magnum Smith & Wesson Model 629—pretty close to being the one I told you I remembered shooting. Only now . . . now that I think about it . . . the one I fired was different. It wasn't stainless steel, I don't think. I . . ."

Frost carried his drink and the Model 629 to a reading chair in the corner of the study and sat down, setting his drink on a small table next to the chair, letting the six-inch barreled .44 rest across his lap. His eye was starting to sting and he could feel the beginnings of a monumental headache taking shape. "I don't know, Monica. Whatever it was that made me forget everything, it had to be some kind of terrible shock. That sounds stupid. But it doesn't matter. Whatever it was—I've got to remember it." He rubbed his right hand over the back of his head as the first jolt of pain erupted. "Damn! If only it didn't hurt so much for me to remember!"

Monica was beside him then, holding him, pressing the side of his face to her breasts. "There's been enough pain for one day, don't you think?" Her fingers caressed the back of his head, stroked his neck. "You can find more

76

pieces to your puzzle tomorrow, darling." She leaned over and kissed him—long and hard and full. She stood up and held out her hand. "Let's go upstairs, can we?"

The one-eyed man stood up beside her, but his eye and his consciousness lingered elsewhere for an instant—on the gun so much like the one in his flashback.

Chapter Nine

By virtue of its size alone, the exterior of Monica's so-called cottage had impressed him. And that had been late at night, with only the headlights from the Ford for illumination. Now the morning sun shone down from an uncharacteristically clear sky, and with Frost viewing Monica's home by the light of day, he had to admit that the place reminded him more of a palace than anything else.

Well rested, a full breakfast under his belt, and with his clothes completely washed and pressed and ready for him to wear when he woke up—Frost felt more at peace with himself than since the whole miserable business of not knowing who he was began.

"Are you with me?" Monica asked, taking Frost's hand and squeezing it gently.

"I'm probably letting myself in for a broken back," the one-eyed man groaned in jest. "But—yeah, I'm ready. I wish I knew for sure if I've ever ridden before."

"Don't worry about that," Monica laughed, her

cheeks blushing at the same time. "From what I saw last night, I'm certain you'll be able to ride just fine. Let's go. The paddock's around in back."

"Last night? Riding? Just what the hell does that mean?" he laughed.

Walking, they followed a stone path leading to the stables, the sounds of horses on the morning air, Frost thinking to himself that perhaps the woman was right. The tension from the past couple of days had been bad on his nerves, and going horseback riding would serve as a refreshing change of pace—sort of a pressure valve.

The horses were saddled and waiting for them when they reached the paddock—Monica explained that the strawberry roan was to be hers; Frost's horse was a dark brown male, that obvious when it went erect for an instant. It was the elderly house servant, Graham, who was handling the reins of the horses.

"Good morning, Graham," Monica greeted.

"Madam," Graham cordially returned, shifting his eyes to the left to take Frost in too. "Sir."

"Morning," Frost smiled.

Monica accepted the reins for the roan, stroking the side of the animal's neck. "Did you encounter any difficulties with the car last night, Graham?"

"None whatsoever, madam," the old man reported, passing Frost the reins to his horse. "Will you be out long, madam?"

Monica inserted her left foot into the appropriate stirrup, grasped the horn and pommel in her hands, and pulled herself up, in a single graceful move, into the saddle—one very similar to the Western saddle on Frost's horse. Monica was wearing a pair of boots and

79

blue jeans, with a white blouse and sleeveless down jacket. "I would think we should be back in two hours' time."

"Very well, madam. I shall prepare tea and biscuits in anticipation of your arrival."

And with that Graham turned and started away.

"Well?" Monica looked down at Frost with a smile. "You can't ride Tornado if you're not on him."

"Tornado?" Frost grinned. "Right." He gripped the pommel and horn, braced his left foot in the stirrup and helped himself aboard. "See. Nothing to it." He held the reins loosely, applying gentle pressure with his knees to the horse's sides, urging the animal forward. "I'm an old cowhand," he sang in an off-key drawl, "from the Rio Grande."

"Careful," Monica warned. "You don't want to spook the horses."

"Ha ha," the one-eyed man laughed. "Very funny."

As a precaution, as well as a means toward jogging his memory, Frost carried the .44 Magnum Model 629, the gun and the Bianchi Phantom shoulder holster both owned by the late Jonathan Hewlett-Jones. Though the holster fit comfortably beneath his bomber jacket, Frost couldn't help thinking in the back of his mind that the Phantom wasn't the holster he usually wore. Try as he might, though, he couldn't remember what kind of holster that other one was.

It was peaceful riding with her, the morning sky so blue, the air so fresh and clean. Nothing was going to happen.

Still mounted they walked the horses over a low, grassy hill, making for a wooded area that began, Frost estimated, a quarter mile away. Tornado, the stallion he was riding, had turned out to be quite an easy ride, prompting Frost to believe that this wasn't the first time he'd ridden a horse.

"It's beautiful out here," Frost observed. "It's like having your own personal paradise to come to. I liked your apartment, but if I had a place like this you'd never get me away from it."

"I could arrange for that," she smiled, then looked away.

Frost held up his right hand, pulling back on the reins with his left, bringing the animal under him to a jolting halt. "What's that?"

"I don't hear any— Wait, you're right. I do hear something."

"Would anybody be mowing out there or, ahh—"

"No," she answered, the pupils of her eyes frightened dots.

The sound in the background was growing louder. "Hurry up! We gotta ride—now!"

"But . . . ?"

"Ride!"

"Gyaagh!" Monica shouted, kicking the roan's sides, sending it galloping further down the hill in a dash for the trees.

"Hyaagh!" Frost yelled, imitating Monica's movements, his heels spurring the stallion ahead, after Monica, his feet dug deep into the stirrups, giving the animal free rein to run. Frost crouched low, knees hugging the saddle, his face close over the animal's darkly flowing mane.

Then, halfway to the cover of the trees, Frost stole a backward glance over his shoulder just as the source of the engine noise crested the hill and started down after them. It was a Land Rover—open canopied and carrying three assault-rifle-armed men in addition to the driver.

Frost turned away, kicking his heels against the animal's sides, the horse galloping faster over the uneven ground. Frost saw Monica was well ahead of him, almost into the trees. Automatic weapons fire then, coming from the Land Rover, Frost wrapping his arms tighter around the horse's neck, riding lower, letting himself go, leaning into the motion.

In his mind Frost saw a picture. Another place. Another time. It was late at night and he was being chased. He was riding a horse bareback. There was a sword in his right hand and he could tell that he was naked. Everyone wanted to kill him. There were more sounds of gunfire and the picture from his past dissolved.*

He squinted his eye against the pain—a desert, but water nearby. A helicopter—an incredibly old man on horseback, a bizarre rifle in his hands, Frost seeing his own silhouette and the silhouette of the animal he rode against the bleached brownness of the ground.**

More gunfire. A blond-haired woman riding with him—he loved her, he somehow realized. The pain—the one-eyed man screamed with it.***

And he was back on the hill again, racing for the trees, the dull aching growing at the back of his head. Monica was in front of him, astride the roan, riding through the edge of the woods, the Land Rover behind them gaining as he looked back, assault rifle fire seemingly everywhere. And suddenly Frost knew he wasn't going to make

*See THEY CALL ME THE MERCENARY #13, Naked Blade, Naked Gun
**See THEY CALL ME THE MERCENARY #15, The Afghanistan Penetration
***See THEY CALL ME THE MERCENARY #3, Fourth Reich Death Squad

it, pulling on the reins, shouting "Whoa!" to the stallion, stopping the horse, somehow keeping his balance and not tumbling off. Frost jerked the reins to his left, bringing the horse around, the one-eyed man's right hand flashing beneath his jacket, finding the Model 629 in the shoulder rig, the .44 Magnum in his fist. Frost swung the stainless S&W revolver on target, aiming at the rapidly advancing Land Rover.

Frost's finger double-actioned the 629's trigger once, the recoil making his wrist scream. But he fired again, then again, the animal bucking under him. Two of the shots plowed into the Land Rover's driver—he could see the body twitch, see it lifting up, the body flipping back. Shot number three crashed into the gas tank, igniting the fuel there, exploding, bodies and parts of bodies flying everywhere, the Land Rover airborne for an instant, then obscured by an orange and black fireball.

The animal jolted, bucked again, rearing back on his hind legs. Frost was falling, unable to hold on, dropping back, hitting the ground, rolling with the fall, pain burning in the back of his head. . . .

The images were real. He was under attack again. The armed men, the ones who maybe were soldiers, chasing him, trying to kill him. The .44 Magnum was in his hand, a belching tongue of flame, a pain in his wrist, a man going down. Then the big handgun was gone and Frost was back at the edge of the cliff, staring at death, the faces of his enemies swimming before him. Another face, too—this of a woman. Someone he should know, but her face was concealed, hidden by shadows. Shots ringing out then, the pain in his head—he was falling again. Falling . . .

Frost shook his head, the vision of the shadowy

woman's face disappearing as he opened his eye. Monica was there, cradling his head, holding him, helping him rise and get back on his feet.

Frost stood, wiping a stinging bead of sweat from his eye, the burning wreckage of the Land Rover scattered across the ground. "Did we get 'em, kid?"

"We got 'em."

Frost could see Monica begin to shake as he took her into his arms. "We're OK now. We're gonna be all right."

"I'm afraid." Her body shook; Frost thought she could be crying. "What are we going to do? Tell me. I need to know. Please tell me."

"We'll do what we have to do to stay alive, Monica. And as soon as we get back to your place I'm phoning the police. The hell with this all."

Chapter Ten

The horses were tethered to a cast-iron hitching post near the side of Monica's house; Frost and the woman were running up the walk leading to the main entrance when the large double doors slammed open and Frost saw the man with an FN FAL assault rifle step outside.

"End of the line, chum," the man gripping the rifle announced, easing the weapon forward. There was no time to go for the 629. Frost and Monica backed across the walk and away from the house. "When we heard the explosion it was agreed that our friends in the Land Rover had failed and that you had succeeded in escaping your fate for an unprecedented third time." The man laughed, his face a leering mask. "Well, your ticket's up now, mate." He jabbed the FN FAL in Frost's direction. "Awright—hands high and keep 'em there." He regarded Monica. "You, too, missy. Alun?"

"Oui?" A second man, armed similarly to the first, stepped from the doorway as Frost watched, spotting a third gunman inside the doorway, standing guard over Graham and a couple of maids.

"Hands up, I told you!"

"Bullshit—gonna kill me anyway. Why the fuck should I listen to you!"

"Alun," the first man snapped. "Check our one-eyed friend here for surprises."

Alun—a thin man with curly hair and an exaggerated overbite—nodded curtly to the first man, slinging his rifle over his shoulder. "Right."

Then, with the first man's FN FAL's muzzle unwavering, Frost remained motionless while the .44 Magnum was found and then taken from him. The man named Alun, holding the S&W Model 629, stepped away. "Only one surprise on him, Keith," he said, holding the handgun aloft. "Only one."

The first man—the apparent leader—sneered, indicating the confiscated .44 with a brief flick of his eyes. "That cannon might've saved your hide, Yank, but it's finished for you now. You've given us quite a chase, taken out some pretty sharp people—I'll grant you that much—but now you're going to get the bullet we thought you got before."

With an almost pleasant-looking smile on his face, the man calmly raised the FN FAL; Frost watched transfixed for an instant.

"No!" Monica screamed the word from Frost's side, throwing herself between them, the rifle discharging, Monica taking the burst, going down, her auburn-colored hair streaming to the side of her head as she fell, falling backward, her eyes staring at Frost—the one-eyed man seeing it all in frame-by-frame slow motion.

The pain in his head was unbearable, the back of his head was exploding with it as Monica struck the walkway, her beautiful face—suffering—alternating with the shadowy image of the woman he'd seen in the flashback. Then the muscles of Monica's face went smooth. Frost saw she was dead.

"Bastard!" Frost jumped forward, on his left foot, his right foot driving up into a high kick, over and across, smashing into the leader's assault rifle, knocking the FN FAL from his grasp. Frost came out of his high kick, wheeling right, lunging for Alun and the .44 Magnum, grabbing Alun's wrist, twisting it, breaking it, Alun cursing as the .44 fell free. Frost caught the Model 629 stock first, his fist curling around it, his right index finger finding the .44's trigger, pulling it, thunder booming like a nightmare from the gun as Alun's face mushroomed into a spray of bone chips, brains and blood.

Frost wheeled left, the third man—the one guarding Graham and the rest—leaping through the doorway. Twice Frost's hand bucked with the recoil of the handgun—one slug ripping away part of the gunman's left shoulder, the second gouging its way into the chest, flopping the man off his feet and onto his back.

Footsteps to his left. The leader—Keith. Frost raised the .44, took aim and fired. Nothing. The hammer fell on an empty chamber. Frost was running then, throwing the .44 into a hedge, gaining on Keith, Frost's feet leaving the ground, his body arcing through the air, hammering against the man, both men spilling to the driveway, rolling across the pavement, Frost losing his grip as Keith shook himself free and got to his feet. Frost did the same.

"Nowhere to run now, you son of a bitch!" Frost rasped.

"No need to, Yank!" the man spit back, his right hand

87

whipping to a sheath at his belt, coming back with a Fairbairn-Sykes pattern commando knife. "I'm gonna cut you up into little pieces!"

The man closed the distance between him and Frost, feinting a stab to the right, then a slash in and to the left, testing Frost's reflexes, searching for an opening.

"I've seen kids better than you," Frost snarled.

"Damn you, Yank!" Keith screamed, making a waistband backhand slash toward Frost's stomach. Frost jumped back, wrenching the narrow trouser belt clear of the loops of his slacks, stretching the belt taut as Keith recovered, then started a downward stabbing hack, the belt vibrating with the impact as it caught the wrist, Frost looping the left end of the belt—the tongue—around the knuckles and the hilt, taking a half step to the right as he twisted the knife hand out and away, Frost's right elbow smashing up. The elbow impacted Keith's nose, breaking it, sending it stabbing up through the ethmoid bone. Keith's knife slipped from the suddenly limp fingers, the eyes wide open in death as the body fell away.

Frost unwound his belt and stuck it in the pocket of his jacket, starting for the house.

He picked up one of the FN FALs in case there were more men about Monica's place. He kept moving.

Easing his way past Graham and the others, Frost set down the rifle, knelt and held Monica's body in his arms, tears burning his eye as he kissed her forehead, then thumbed closed her eyes. "Thank you," he whispered softly.

The bombs were going off in his head again. Steadily larger explosions, the pain excruciating as he lowered Monica's body to the walkway and staggered to his feet.

"Phone the police," he rasped to Graham, then turned

and stumbled past the weeping maids, over the bodies of the men he had killed, his head pounding uncontrollably as he made his way through the double doorway and into the house. He was in the foyer then, floaters flying across his eye, feeling like he was about to black out, starting to fall, catching himself on the edge of a table, the morning edition of *The Guardian* on top of the table. Page one. A follow-up to the story of the missing American journalist, Bess Stallman—the woman's photograph next to the story.

"Bess," Frost whispered, his fingers clamping around the edge of the table as he raised his face to the mirror on the wall behind the table. "Hank Frost," he told the reflection, a fresh spasm of pain pulling him under, the death scene from his flashbacks replaying now in graphic detail—at the brink of the cliff, the armed men dressed like soldiers, one of them raising his weapon to kill, firing at him, Bess suddenly there and screaming, taking the bullet meant for him, O'Hara nearby, but unable to help. Then black water and hands reaching for him, something dragging him under, fighting, battling, then surrendering. Darkness. Relief.

Chapter Eleven

"Captain Frost?"

The one-eyed man was half asleep.

"Captain Frost—can you hear me?" The voice was coming to him from another galaxy. "Captain?"

"Yeah, yeah—all right, already—I'm awake." Frost slowly opened his eye, focusing on his surroundings, sensing immediately that he was out of the clothes Monica had bought him, wearing a pair of pajamas instead. He was stretched flat on a bed, his head resting on a pillow, covered up to his chin by a sheet. A thermal blanket was over the sheet and he was warm. He was in a room, small and gray, with a window—blinds drawn—to his left beside the bed. He took a deep breath and smells translating to disinfectant and medicine came to his mind. "Hospital?"

"Yes, Captain—you're in a hospital," the owner of the voice confirmed.

"But how did . . . ?" Frost rolled his head across the pillow to his right and stopped as a flicker of recognition came to him from the past. "Ah—Inspector Thurmond?"

The florid-faced man sitting in a hardwood chair close to the bed smiled. "Inspector Thurmond—yes." His accent was mildly Scottish. "I'm pleased to see you haven't forgotten me."

"Carlotta Fleisch and her gang of terrorists—yeah, I remember." Frost shifted on the bed, the back of his head feeling stiff and sore. "That was when I thought Bess had been . . ." He didn't say the word.*

The inspector sighed, leaning forward in his seat. "Aye, man—I can imagine how it is to remember that now. And it appears we're meeting again under painfully similar circumstances."

The one-eyed man frowned. "Bess and O'Hara," Frost told him.

"I'm afraid so. And that's why I've been on your trail ever since you, Miss Stallman, and your friend from the FBI were reported missing. I heard about the disappearance through communication channels in my office in Glasgow. Because you and I had worked together before, I di' no' have much trouble arranging a temporary duty transfer to London and Scotland Yard." He made a clicking noise at the side of his mouth. "I do no' think they were that displeased to take advantage of my services. If the truth were known—the Yard was just as much in the dark about the three of you vanishing as anyone else."

Frost swallowed, licked his lips, then asked, "Then how did you know I was in London?"

"At first I didn't, but when the bodies of the men who were trying to kill you started popping up with alarming regularity—I knew for a fact you were out and about."

"Hah—flattery'll get you nowhere."

*See THEY CALL ME THE MERCENARY #9, The Terror Contract

"It's not that, Captain, I assure you, but knowing a bit of your professional background as I do, it wasn't that difficult to determine that the party responsible for leaving such a trail to follow had to be a specialist such as yourself. From the four men you left down Whitechapel way, to the bunch you took out in Hyde Park, all clues pointed to you."

Frost grumbled, frustrated. "So where's that leave us? My memory's all shot to hell."

"The amnesia—I know. I've read a statement from a . . . Doctor Titchen, I believe his name was."

"Yeah—a cowboy, neat old guy. Friend of—of Monica."

"I'm sorry about her, lad—I am." He cleared his throat. "At any rate, Doctor Titchen's prognosis of your condition has been substantiated by physicians here at the hospital. The apparent bullet wound to your head was superficial. To the matter at hand, though, Captain—I must ask you to tell me exactly how much you remember."

"I know who I am, for starters. I also remember Bess being shot. And when I woke up, I recognized you. Most of my past is pretty clear. Then there's everything that happened to me since I came to in that alley with my pockets empty and no place to go. Most of that, I'd like to forget—but not all of it." Frost needed a cigarette. "How I got to that alley—hell if I know. I know I was with Bess and O'Hara and we were attacked by some guys who might have been soldiers. For some reason, O'Hara wasn't able to use his Model 29, so I was using it. That's about when things go all fuzzy around the edges. Bess stopped a bullet meant for me—that I'm sure of. Then I think there was more shooting and there was this pain in my head. After that I was . . . After that, nothing," he

92

shrugged. "I know it's all there, but I can't seem to grab hold of it." The cotton-dryness of his mouth made him wish for a drink. "I'm sorry, Inspector. That's all I can remember."

"Very good, Captain." The inspector drew his chair nearer Frost's bed, speaking in low, almost conspiratorial sounding tones. "I won't mince words, Captain Frost. There's no reason to. You perhaps better than any of us have an idea of what we're up against, and we need your help. Your fiancee was working on a story that, we believe, got her predecessor killed. At this point in time it is indeed possible that Miss Stallman is . . . is dead. But the blackguards responsible for the deed are still out there somewhere, part of a well-organized, ruthless organization. For all we know they could be terrorists. You're in a unique situation in that respect, Captain. You've met the enemy firsthand, and lived to walk away. So many men wouldn't be sent to kill you if you didn't possess some piece of information that they don't want revealed. The location of their base of operations? The total number of their force? A conspiracy in the works—I don't know. But whatever it is, it's trapped inside your brain, Captain. And somehow we need to release it. We need to have you remember."

"Don't think I haven't tried. Shit—I didn't even know who I was. This amnesia thing . . . And I don't think it's all tied in together with me getting shot in the head, either. I think the fact that I witnessed Bess taking the shot meant for me has just as much to do with my memory going. The shock of the two things combined is what did it to me, maybe."

"Certainly the trauma of seeing Miss Stallman shot has affected you." Inspector Thurmond's jaw jutted forward. "Hell, man, a shock like that would tear apart the strongest of us. But you said yourself that, at first, you didn't know who you were. And now you do. That means your memory's coming back. And it also means that, if we work hard enough at it, we stand a damned good chance of unlocking the rest of the secrets you've got tucked away up there," and he jabbed his index finger at Frost. "I'm asking you, Captain, can you help us, man?"

"Bess and O'Hara. Monica died because she didn't look away when I was in trouble. Hell—you can open my head with a can opener if it'll nail those bastards."

"Good, man!" The inspector stood, straightening the lapels of his coat, nodding politely to Frost. "I'll call on you in the morning, then. You leave here at nine o'clock. Oh, and try and get plenty of rest. And if you're concerned about security—well, don't be," Thurmond added as he reached the door. "There will be two men posted outside your room at all times—armed men."

"Thanks, Inspector," Frost told him.

The door opened and closed. Frost was tired. His eye closed.

Chapter Twelve

Frost wiped his mouth with the napkin. "Hey—listen. My compliments to the chef, huh? That's the first time I've ever had braised bicycle tire."

The woman, a young girl in her early twenties and wearing a hospital uniform, was grinning. "What a lot of cheek you've got. That was a perfectly good supper. Far sight better than the one I had."

"You have my sympathy." Frost felt a gurgle rumbling across his stomach. "Really, the supper was fine. Only next time tell the chef to go easy on the air pressure. I'll be lucky tonight if I don't sleep on the ceiling."

"You're a funny one, aren't you?" she laughed, lifting the tray from Frost's bed and setting it on the night table to his left. "You should be grateful."

"How's that—you could've made me eat two plates of the stuff?"

"No not that at all. I mean you should be grateful that you're here in a room by yourself. Not many here get that privilege—you can believe that. Most everyone else stays in one of our large wards, no privacy at all."

She turned and went to a cart with a small plastic tub at the top, the cart parked near the door to his room. She wheeled the cart over beside the bed and quickly pulled off the blanket and sheet covering him, leaving it bunched up at the foot of the bed.

"Hey!" Frost protested.

"Hush, you'll be all right." She removed a lid off the top of the plastic tub on the cart and reached inside, removing a bright yellow sponge, dripping with water.

"What's that for?" Frost asked, suspicious.

"For your bath, of course." The girl gripped the sponge in both hands, wringing it out over the tub. "Please take off your pajamas."

"Now, wait a . . ."

"We can start with just the tops, if you like, but it's all going to get done in the end. Now, hurry—otherwise the water's going to get cold."

"Nuts." Frost sat up in the bed, unbuttoned the pajama tops and slipped them off. "There."

She began washing him down with the sponge.

"Listen, Nurse—"

"It's Sister. Sister Davis," she corrected.

"Sister?" Frost almost choked. "You don't look a thing like any nun I've ever seen."

"I'm not a nun." She worked the sponge over his chest. "You're an American so you wouldn't know, but that's how it is in England. You start out being a nurse, then you get promoted to being a sister. Right now I'm a sister."

"And what's after that," Frost joked, "a brother?"

"No." She dipped the sponge into the tub, wringing it out again before continuing. "After a sister, the next step up is matron. Not many make it that far. A matron's sort of an overseer of all the nurses and sisters. Please turn over."

"Really?" Frost said, doing as he was told—not liking it. He'd been in an English hospital before—no one had ever explained chain of command to him.

He felt it as she worked the sponge deep into the muscles of his back. "See, you do like it."

She moved the sponge higher, washing his neck and shoulders. "You seem pretty casual about it—having just one eye and all, I mean."

"Why not?" he admitted. "Grumbling about it's not going to get me seeing stereo all of a sudden."

"That's true enough," and she dipped the sponge back into the water and began washing his lower back. He could hear the water dribbling. "If you don't mind my asking . . . ?" She let the question hang in the air.

"How I lost my eye?" Frost asked, picking up the cue he had been given. "You really want to know?"

"If you don't mind. Matron would be upset if she knew that I'd asked, but I am curious. Well?"

"Nothing much to it," Frost began. "It all happened back when I was in college. As you can probably imagine, I was an extremely bright student—the smartest one on campus, now that I think about it."

"And the most conceited," Sister Davis put in.

"That's beside the point," Frost confessed, getting back to the tale. "Anyway, I was an English major: the classics, prepositions, and verbs—that sort of thing. But deep down inside me I always harbored a strong interest in science. Well, as it turned out, the annual science fair was coming up, and I decided to enter. I had always fancied myself—"

"I can believe that," she said.

"Ah, I had always fancied myself something of an amateur astronomer, so when it came down to the nuts and bolts of picking a project, my choice was a natural. I wanted to build a working model of our solar system. The science fair was less than two weeks away, which meant that I had to spend most of my days, and half of my nights painting, gluing, and slapping the project together. But in the end it was worth it. Wow! The day the science fair opened my pride and joy was ready to be judged with the best of them."

"I thought this was about how you lost your eye?" the girl questioned, dropping the sponge in the tub of water on the cart as he looked over his shoulder at her, then tapping him gently on the back. "Clean as a whistle. Now slip your bottoms off and let me do the rest."

"Aw, really," Frost rolled over and sat up, "I don't think this is necessary—I'll be outa here tomorrow— take a shower then. Honest, kid."

"I shouldn't like to have to ring for Matron," Sister Davis was smiling. "Besides, I'm sure you'll enjoy the rest of the bath just as much as the first part—maybe even more."

Frost shrugged, raising up on his elbows and skinning out of the pajama bottoms.

"You needn't be upset," she reassured, taking up the sponge and beginning to bathe him below the waist. "I'm not going to bite you."

"If you say so. Now—where was I?"

"The day the science fair opened . . ."

"Oh, yeah. Well, I was exhibit number six in line to be judged. The judges were making their way down to where I was sitting, about to exhibit number four, I guess, when I thought it would be a good idea to plug in my project and get everything revolving around the sun. It all worked beautifully, and I'm sure I would've won first place if the delicate wiring inside the motor of my project hadn't picked that precise moment to short circuit. It was terrible. One minute I had a perfectly operating replica of the solar system, the next—total chaos. Normally with a short circuit, you'd expect that the motor would've shut down, but instead of that happening, the motor in my project speeded up, throwing everything in orbit around my model of the sun at least a hundred times too fast. The judges were already taking a look at exhibit number five, so I knew if I was going to salvage my entry, I was going to have to hurry. I bent down to see if there was anything I could do to get my project back to normal. Then it happened—Mars tore away from its orbit and hit me right in my left eye. That was bad enough, but then Jupiter broke away and hit Mars, pushing it even deeper into my eye. By the time Neptune got into the act, Mars was there, and my left eye wasn't. And the sad part of it all was that I didn't even get an honorable mention from the judges."

"What a tragic story. And how's Uranus?" she laughed. "But if you ask me, I think that with a little precaution, the accident could have been prevented."

"Maybe," Frost agreed. "All I know is that getting unexpectedly hit in the eye with Mars was no fun at all. I certainly didn't planet that way."

She didn't laugh.

After his sponge bath, Frost was given a tiny paper cup of medication. "It will help you sleep," Sister Davis explained. "A few minutes after you drink it, you won't be able to keep your funny eye open. You'll be asleep before you know it." She smiled and left.

The gooey, green-colored liquid she had given him to drink tasted bad. He closed his eye. . . .

Always it was the same. The soldiers, the men dressed in military uniforms. They were attacking, charging at him, repeatedly trying to kill him. O'Hara was there, but Frost couldn't see him. And all the while the one-eyed man fought, driving back hordes of his attackers with O'Hara's massive N-Frame.

Frost was standing on the brink of the tallest cliff in the world, the heels of his sixty-five-dollar shoes hanging over the edge, his sense of balance all but gone. He faced a wall of soldiers—one of the uniformed men raised a gun, flexed his finger over the trigger, caressing it, jerking his finger back, firing at Frost as Bess appeared out of nowhere, again and again, a hundred times over, taking the bullet meant for him.

He saw Bess drop, collapsing to the ground as pain stitched its way across the side of his head. And he was falling, too—spilling off of the cliff and floating down in a spiralling cartwheel lasting an eternity.

He'd scream and close his eye, and when he opened it—the men were there again. The fighting. Bess dying. The soldiers, Frost blasting away with the Model 29, his heels to the edge of the cliff, and then Bess, always Bess—jumping in front of the soldier with the gun and taking the bullet meant for him, falling to the ground just before the pain. Then the fall.

The falling was lasting longer this time, and this time it was different—no longer dropping through bottomless reaches, but rushing instead to jagged rocks and stones below, moving faster, caught in gravity's merciless grip, plunging down, down, down. He hit the rocks.

Frost opened his eye, the skin under his pajamas wet with cold sweat. He took a deep breath and let it out slowly, his heart hammering in his chest. The dreams—the dreams had been so real. Frost froze.

In the quiet darkness of his room, he was not alone.

100

Chapter Thirteen

The one-eyed man stabbed his left thumb against the bedside nurse-call button and rolled right, his pillow taking two impacts, the movement of a slide that needed oiling all that he could hear, the silenced pistol's coughing sound barely audible, the one-eyed man hitting the floor, starting to move across it.

The door opened, a shaft of yellow light from the corridor washing across the greenish flooring. Frost looked up, a nurse or whatever they were called was standing in the doorway, a glass jar in her left hand, her right hand on the door handle. There was the phut sound, then the grinding of the slide against the frame as the bottle in her hand disintegrated and the woman screamed.

The one-eyed man was up, moving, hurtling his body across the bed toward the black-clad intruder as the gun wheeled toward him, his right hand slapping it out and away, the killer's left hand slamming against the wall, the gun discharging again. Frost mentally counted the shots—four. The shape was that of a Colt Woodsman and the silencer on it looked improvised. Four shots gone, six, possibly seven remaining if his memory served and the Woodsman had a ten-shot magazine.

His left knee smashed up, into the man's gut, the man shoving him back, Frost falling into the bed, his back impacting against the bed frame, the one-eyed man screaming.

The gun—it was coming on line again, the man holding it massive, blocky—big. Frost reared back against his elbows, snapping his right leg up and out toward the gun, his bare toes impacting the silencer, the pistol discharging again. Five shots down.

The gun was still in the killer's grip as the man fell back against the wall, Frost throwing himself forward, his head hammering against the killer's chest, his right hand groping for the pistol, finding it, the pistol discharging again. Six shots gone.

The nurse was still screaming, but the scream was more distant now, from the hallway he guessed; the man he wrestled with against the bedside wall cursed him in Spanish.

"Spanish?" Frost choked on the word as the man hammered a fist into his gut, Frost rocking left, against the cornering wall, still holding the pistol and the gunman's left hand in his right. A knee smash—the one-eyed man saw it, felt it coming, rolled right, letting go of the pistol and heard the scream as the gunman's knee crashed against the wall.

"*Eho de puta!*" the gunman snarled, Frost getting his balance against the bed's headboard, snapping his right foot out, back-kicking, the impact hard on his bare foot as he looked back, the foot slamming hard against the left side of the gunman's head.

There was a shot, the bedding beside Frost taking it.

Seven shots now.

Frost wheeled right, his left hand snatching the bedpan under its lips, then swinging out with it, swatting it, into the killer's face and head and nose, Frost throwing himself against the man, the gun discharging again—twice. Nine shots gone. The window behind him shattered; the killer screamed as Frost's right knee found the squishy area he wanted—testicles.

"*Mierda!*"

"Same to you, asshole," the one-eyed man rasped, ramming the right knee up again, the killer doubling forward.

The pistol discharged, more shattering of glass. Ten shots.

One might still remain.

Frost punched his left hand forward again, still holding the bedpan, the stainless steel grinding at his knuckles, the hollow sound of the bedpan against the gunman's head almost comic.

The pistol—the left arm was moving, the pistol crashing down. Frost was losing his grip; the pistol was hammering against Frost's right shoulder and the right side of his neck—again and again. Frost started to stumble back, then swung his right, feigning, hammering a roundhouse punch outward with his left, still holding the bedpan, catching the Spanish-speaking gunman full in the face, the nose breaking, blood spurting in the yellow light from the open door.

A knee smash—Frost felt it, twisted away, taking it in his pelvis rather than his groin, falling back.

He looked up, moving, but too late—the gun was leveling at him, the chunky silencer almost ridiculous looking.

There was no sound.

The one-eyed man felt himself smile.

The pistol was empty. He couldn't remember if the slide should lock back or not after the last shot—but the gun was empty nonetheless. His left foot snapped out, catching the man below the belt and above the legs. There was a scream. The one-eyed man was on his feet now, his right fist hammering out, then his left, then his right, beating the man back against the wall, his knuckles screaming at him as bone contacted bone.

His left grabbed at the man's clothes, wrenching him forward, his right knee hammering up into a knee smash. The man threw his weight suddenly forward and Frost fell back, the gunman on top of him now, the pistol gone somewhere on the floor, the bed moving under Frost as the gunman lunged against him, the hands on Frost's neck.

Frost's hands—open palmed—slammed against the brute-sized man's ears, but there was just a twitching to the heavy-browed face, a stream of curses in Spanish more fluent than Frost could understand, the bed still moving.

Frost drew his left hand down, then his right, floaters across his eye as the burning tightness in his throat increased. He slammed his left fist against the right side of the killer's head—but there was no distance to build momentum, no weight behind the blow. His right, his right—he repeated it inside himself.

He hammered his right up, under the jaw, snapping the head back, getting his knees up, under the man's vastly greater weight, pushing, the hands still locked on his throat, a coolness on his hands—numbing?

Frost shoved up with all his strength, the body started

to move, up, over him, his hands wrestling back the thumbs that compressed his neck, breaking them, the man screaming, Frost rolling him up and over, Frost rolling with him, the sound of glass shattering, screaming from the gunman, Frost seeing a blur of motion, a weightless feeling, the hands releasing on his neck.

His body shuddered and the motion was stopped for an instant, then began again and he was falling, his face hitting into sharp things that tore at him, slapped at him, made his eye sting.

He lurched forward, fell and stopped.

He pushed himself up on the palms of his hands, looking behind him, over his shoulder. There were those crazy-sounding European police sirens in the background, and white-clad hospital people were running everywhere across a parking lot.

Hands were reaching down to him, but the one-eyed man shook them away, climbing unsteadily to his feet.

Shaking his head.

A Volkswagen bus—the little van type. A hole in the roof, human legs extending up from the hole, the roof partially caved in.

His arms and legs shook as he approached the Volkswagen. It was the gunman—through a side window he could see what was left of the head in the orange light of the emergency flasher.

Hospital people were into the Volkswagen now, trying to get to the man.

Frost felt like telling them not to bother—the one-eyed man knew death when he saw it. He remembered that much.

Chapter Fourteen

He had remembered he liked smoking Camels—he couldn't remember if he'd remembered it before. He sat, smoking through a pack, listening to himself breathe. It was a reassuring sound.

He wore his own clothes—Thurmond had gotten them from the hotel where Frost had stayed with Bess. O'Hara had had the next room.

The one-eyed man cursed himself.

He had spent the rest of the night in a hotel, under heavy guard—so heavily guarded he'd wound up sleeping with two uniformed and—oddly—armed policemen in his room, the policemen presumably wide awake. One of the Scotland Yard guards who had been posted at the hospital had been found with his throat slit, the body in a laundry hamper. The other man was in critical condition with a broken neck, his body found in a linen closet.

The gun had been a Woodsman, the silencer a basement machine-shop model, but effective. There had been no slide lock. Each of the forty-grain slugs had been tipped with ammonia to poison anyone shot with them if the killing weren't done instantly with the bullet itself.

"Argentinean," Thurmond said blandly, coming through the doorway, shutting the frosted glass door behind him.

"What?"

"An Argentine—imported hit man, Captain Frost."

"O'Hara had a gun. Why did O'Hara have a gun, Inspector?"

Thurmond sat down beside the desk rather than behind it, crossing his legs, smoothing his tie. "Sometimes, I suppose, friends can't always tell other friends all they'd like, can they?"

"What the hell does that mean?"

"O'Hara wasn't spending his holiday with you and your Miss Stallman, Captain. Aye, but I'd wager he wishes he had been if he's still alive."

"Maybe I'm still fuzzy, but spell it out, huh?"

"As best I can, Captain, as best I can. But tell me first all you remember about O'Hara and his gun."

Frost stubbed out the Camel, then with the Bic disposable he'd been given, lit another. "All right—let's say he was on some kind of assignment. Then why not the little Chiefs Special he always carried in the ankle holster instead of the big .44? Nothing makes sense."

"Why did Agent O'Hara carry a .44 Magnum—rather a large gun? I fired one once."

"I think he was a little paranoid about not being able to drop something he shot—always got after me about—"

"About what?"

"The gun I carry. The gun I carry!" Frost suddenly remembered the gun he habitually carried. "A Browning High Power—Metalifed. Ron, ahh, Ron Mahovsky made it up for me!"

"Very good, Captain—memory is returning, isn't it? What sort of knife?"

"Ahh," and Frost licked his lips. "A Gerber—Gerber MkI Boot Knife. Never carry it in my boot though—always in . . . in my trouser band, near the small of my back sometimes."

"And you have another gun in Miss Stallman's office safe in England—you were never able to get it out legally, correct? The same as Miss Stallman's Python?"

"Yeah, a little K-Frame—Ron made it for me, too."

"The Yard knew about the guns—and when you do leave England you'll be able to take them with you. What else do you remember?"

"I remember giving Bess that Python—in Africa—right after we first met, so she could stay alive with it."*

"What kind of shoulder holster do you prefer, Captain?"

"Cobra. Ahh, Cobra Comvest."

"And Agent O'Hara?"

"Cattle Baron leather—a big holster. He loves 'em."

"And his ankle gun—how does he carry it?"

"Ankle holster. Cobra, I think—yeah."

"His knife?"

"Doesn't carry one. Not a real knife anyway—just a penknife."

"Good," Thurmond smiled, his eyes twinkling. "Tell me what happened when you saw O'Hara with the gun—the Model 29. The Metalifed Model 29—was it Mag-Na-Ported? And what kind of grips?"

"Pachmayr's—and yeah, it was Mag-Na-Ported—Metalifed—he took it out of the glove compartment."

"But that's impossible. Your car was parked near the hotel, or Miss Stallman's car from the news bureau."

"Yeah, but that thing was so damned little. O'Hara

*See THEY CALL ME THE MERCENARY #1, The Killer Genesis

kept grousing about it—and it was binding up my legs, too, and—"

"And you what, Captain? What did you do?"

Frost stood up, dropping the Camel, still lit, into the ash tray. "Shit! We rented a car—rented a car—a bigger car, damnit!"

"Where? What kind of car? What—"

"Ford. One of the downsized LTDs—real roomy inside though." Frost laughed. "Funny, like pimples."

"Pimples?"

"Yeah. The letter "m" on the sign, it was screwed up—faded or something. Should have read something else—"

"Wha—what should it have read, Captain?"

"It said Acne—like the pimples."

"Acme—Acme Car Letting?"

Frost was tired, his breath coming pantingly to him. "Ahh—"

"Agent O'Hara was—you have a lovely Americanism—bird-dogging. He was bird-dogging your Miss Stallman for the FBI. The murder-for-hire ring she was investigating, the investigation her predecessor was involved with before he died in the accident—it was perhaps related to a similar ring in the United States. I can tell ya why it was he carried his .44 Magnum, lad—the men he was up against meant business. Killers."

Thurmond turned away, lighting a pipe with a match with one hand, picking up the telephone with his left. "Thurmond here—aye—a lead finally. Acme Car Letting—whatever the blue blazes they call themselves. Acme something and they let cars for hire. Find them, and quick."

Frost closed his eye, his head aching. And he was very tired.

Chapter Fifteen

"I know, you wrecked the bloody car!" the chunky, slightly wall-eyed woman behind the counter almost shrieked as her eyes—as best they apparently could—locked on his face.

"A light blue LTD with a missing hubcap. O'Hara rented it—"

"The fast-talking Yank rented it, but where is it?" she demanded, Frost crossing the dirty-yellow-painted office to the counter, the counter littered with sales receipts the woman had been sorting when he and Thurmond had walked in.

"You rented the bloody thing for four days at the most—been more than a week, it 'as!"

"Madam," Thurmond interjected, flashing his I.D. "Scotland Yard has greater things to worry about concerning this gentleman, his friend, and the blond-haired woman who accompanied them."

"The blondie from the papers! Coo!"

"Bess—you remember her then?" Frost asked the woman, leaning across to her over the counter, smelling

110

her breath—garlic—and edging back slightly.

"Now that I see you. Ain't every day we get someone in 'ere with an eye patch like some bloody pirate."

The woman smiled now.

"Madam, the Yard shall endeavor to recover the lost vehicle. But we cannot without further information."

"I reported it stolen two days ago, I did!"

Thurmond turned to the other man with them—a plain-clothes officer named Lowrey. "Peter, check the local people—see what they have on the light blue Ford. Get it all, then get the license, make, description—the part about the missing hubcap—all of it on the wire immediately."

Frost leaned across the counter—he kissed the loud-mouthed, wall-eyed woman on the cheek.

She smiled.

Chapter Sixteen

Frost sipped at the Myers's Rum—he liked other things better than O'Hara's favorite drink but, somehow, his memory was all tied in to Mike O'Hara and he drank the rum in hopes of jogging it. Thurmond sat across from him, their food half eaten, the club not one to which Thurmond belonged, but Thurmond there as a guest of his direct supervisor in the Yard, Frost in turn Thurmond's guest. "My own club in Scotland," Thurmond mentioned through a mouthful of steak and kidney pie. "Aye—the food is better."

"You read minds?"

"The food?"

"No, about the club."

"I wish I could, but I dunno anyone who can do that, Captain. You remembering anything yet?"

Frost laughed. "It's not like washing your socks, ya know—"

"Aye—that I do. But I need you to remember," and Thurmond downed another mouthful of food, washing it down with water from the crystal tumbler beside his plate.

"Now, laddie, think for me—when O'Hara drew his gun from the glove compartment of the blue LTD—what shade of blue again?"

"Light blue," Frost nodded.

"Aye—light blue it was. What else was in the glove compartment?"

"Some speedloaders—180-grain JHPs in 'em."

"For the Model 29, I take it. I'm no expert on guns."

"Yeah," Frost sighed.

"Understand there are different brands of the things—the speedloaders. What kind were his, do you know?"

Frost thought for a moment, chewing at a mouthful of steak. The steak was all right but he'd eaten better.

"What kind, Captain Frost?"

"Safariland," Frost told him.

"They make holsters, too, don't they?" Thurmond nodded, not waiting for an answer. "So what was it that prompted O'Hara to take his Metalifed Model 29 and his speedloaders from the glove compartment?"

"We—we saw something."

"You and Bess Stallman? You and O'Hara? Who? All three of you?"

"Yes."

"Who saw it first?"

"Bess. She was looking out the window."

"Where was she sitting?"

"Between us—between Mike and—"

"So she was looking out the windshield?"

"Yes."

"It was in front of you then, and O'Hara was driving."

"He leaned across Bess and I opened the glove com-

113

partment for him. He wouldn't tell me why he had the gun—he just grinned and made some crack, like he always does." Frost swallowed a mouthful of food—he hadn't chewed it. "Or did."

"Aye—but the faster we remember, the faster we know—the faster *you* remember, lad. Think—what was it Bess saw that made O'Hara go for his gun?"

Frost's head ached. "I—ahh, I don't—"

"What happened after he got his gun out of the glove compartment?" Thurmond interrupted.

"We started off through the woods. I was worried about Bess being with us. I was complaining to Mike."

"To Agent O'Hara?"

"Yeah—to Agent O'Hara. I was complaining to him that we should have sent Bess back. He said we couldn't—might be all over the place."

"What? What might be all over the place?"

"I don't—ahh, shit," and Frost threw his fork down on the plate. He looked up past Thurmond; the other men in the club—even the waiters—were staring at him. Frost grinned at the waiter nearest him. "The fork was dirty," he told him.

The waiter rushed over, took the fork and in what seemed less than ten seconds was back with a fresh one, then left.

Frost continued eating.

"What was all over the place now?" Thurmond asked again.

"I don't know," Frost answered—quietly this time.

"What happened while you walked through the woods with O'Hara and Bess?"

Frost touched his right cheek. "I scratched myself—on a tree branch, I think. Bess—she took a handkerchief and cleaned the cut. She said I was acting like a baby about it—but it hurt," Frost smiled. "But not after she fixed it."

Thurmond smiled, looked down at his plate thoughtfully and speared more food with his fork. He looked up as he held the fork, not eating yet. "What happened after Bess Stallman fixed your cheek where you cut it on the branch, Captain Frost?"

The one-eyed man laughed. "This is stupid—'cause it was a clear day—pretty outside, you know?"

"What's stupid?"

"Fog. The fog—it was from nowhere. Maybe it's just in my head," Frost laughed, taking another swallow of the Myers's Rum.

"What happened once the fog was there?" Thurmond said, his voice old sounding, tired sounding.

"The fog—O'Hara got sick. We saw these soldiers," Frost almost whispered. "Mike couldn't use his gun—I don't remember why, maybe because he was sick, but I don't remember why he was sick. But I took it." The pain burned in his head again, Frost taking a pull on the glass of Myers's Rum again. He closed his eye, talking as he did. "Somewhere down the line there were the soldiers again. And somebody else had Mike's .44 Mag. He was shooting at me. Bess—she took the shot and—"

"And?" he heard Thurmond's voice ask.

"And I'm falling," Frost told him, opening his eye. "Freud would have loved me, wouldn't he," the one-eyed man smiled. He didn't close his eye. He was afraid—terrified—that he'd see Bess die.

Chapter Seventeen

He'd stopped drinking the rum, eaten heavily, had a
heavy dessert—two pieces of chocolate cake—and drunk
a good deal of coffee. The end result—unintentional or,
at the best, subconscious—was stone-cold sobriety. The
hotel had looked old and quite beautifully built as they
had pulled up, the lobby deserted—Frost assumed
because of the hour. Frost, with only an overnight bag,
had been accompanied by Thurmond to the room, a suite
on the sprawling west wing of the old place—at least
Thurmond had said it was the west wing. Two bottles had
been in the top drawer of the dresser—Boodles Gin and
Jack Daniels Black Label. Frost had selected the Jack
Daniels even before Thurmond had left for the night,
pledging to return in the morning and also pledging Frost
a quiet night. Scotland Yard's anti-terrorist flying-squad
people were on duty throughout the building. Nothing
could harm Frost short of a bomb—and it would have to
be a large bomb, Thurmond had winked, leaving.

Frost sat now, watching a commercial television

station, an old Ronald Reagan movie playing. Frost watched the television, sipping at the Jack Daniels. The president, his battered cowboy hat partially concealing a smile, was apparently the local lawman. There was a gunfight coming. "You can get those suckers, sir," Frost intoned, watching.

He took another sip of the Jack, drinking, watching the movie, trying not to see Bess die in front of his eye when he closed it, trying not to remember. It was late—he should be in bed, he told himself. But then he'd dream, and he didn't want that. He would avoid sleep until he couldn't avoid it, make himself so tired that dreaming wouldn't come, not conscious dreaming anyway. He didn't want to see it again.

The president was ready—and so were the bad guys.

The gunfight was going to erupt any minute.

It did—but the gunfire the one-eyed man heard was from beyond the door.

"Holy shit," he rasped, the door bursting inward, his hand grabbing for the bottle of Jack Daniels, the television sputtering off, the lights going as well. Smoke and a solitary belching of flame puffed through the open doorway. He felt the Jack Daniels running down his sleeve.

It would be the soldiers from his flashbacks, or perhaps the London crooks—there was a secondary shock. It would be the soldiers. The old hotel in Kent had been as well guarded as a fortress—he had believed Thurmond about that. To be bombed, to be invaded—there was more of the gunfire from the hallway—it would have to be a military operation. The cheap-shot gangsters were out—and so were solitary assassins like the Argentinean who had tried to murder him in the hospital. Thurmond

117

had checked the prints and I.D.ed the man as Alfredo Lorca LaCruz. Soldiers, Argentinean hitmen, London gangsters.

His head ached as he righted the bottle, corking it, wishing for a gun, starting toward the corridor doorway, flames visible on the far side. He'd brought no luggage except for a change of underwear, socks and a clean shirt. His electric razor and toothbrush could be replaced. He stopped by the doorway, smoke—acrid and heavy— filling the corridor and penetrating his room, the light of flames all that there was to see by. He was four floors up—his back wouldn't take a jump to the ground, still aching him from the fight in the hospital room when he'd slammed it against the bed.

It would be through the corridor or nothing. He started through the doorway, then tucked back, the gunfire—submachine gun the origin, he guessed—very close.

The one-eyed man tucked back near the door frame, the wall hot behind him, the closed, spilled bottle of Jack Daniels Black Label his only weapon—as yet.

There was a lamp near the doorway. Frost set down the square bottle and grabbed at the lamp, ripping it from its plug in the wall outlet, then tearing the cord away from the lamp. He set the cord on the table beside the bottle of Jack and reached under the shade for the bulb. He unscrewed it, then dropped the lamp to the floor in front of the doorway, partially blocking it. He was ready.

More of the subgun fire, close now, so close that he could imagine at least that he heard the running foot-steps of the men doing the shooting.

The one-eyed man tucked back beside the wall, waiting, almost hoping they'd come before the corridor became impassable with the flames if it wasn't already that way.

He waited, the light bulb on the table beside him, the bottle of Jack there, the lamp's electrical cord twisted in his hands, an improvised garrote.

He needed a gun—so he needed to kill a man to get it.

The man came. He saw the shadow in the reflected firelight, saw the outline of a body coming through the doorway, saw a distinct human shape, a face black-camouflaged or soot stained, a black Navy watchcap covering the head, black, fingerless cloth gloves holding a Sten MkII—like the subguns used in the park. He wished he had one now.

The man stepped through, Frost stepping one long stride forward, his right knee smashing up into the spine between the kidneys, the electrical cord garrote looping over the man's head, Frost wheeling 180 degrees left, holding the garrote in both hands still, hauling the garroted body up and over his right shoulder, flipping it as he doubled over forward, hearing the breaking sound as the neck snapped, then loosing the garrote, letting the body sag down. He started to turn for the subgun—but a second man was coming through the doorway. The one-eyed man reached for the bottle of Jack, the heavy square bottle in his left hand, his right already getting the light bulb. The left hand snaked out, across the face of the second man as he brought up the subgun to fire, the bottle connecting, shattering, the head snapping back, the subgun discharging into the ceiling as Frost stepped right, holding the light bulb by its base, slapping it across the exposed throat of the second man, the bulb breaking, the jagged glass at its edge by the base gouging across the carotid artery, ripping it open, a short duration, garbled

119

scream as the body sagged, the eyes rolling back, bigger seeming against the dark-camouflaged face.

Frost reached down for the second man's subgun—it was the closest. He heard the voice, wanted to vomit. "Not this time, Captain Frost. This time you buy the whole nine yards."

His head ached—and the one-eyed man screamed. He remembered it all, the soldier's face and voice, that of one of the killers in the woods.

"You son of a bitch," the one-eyed man rasped, throwing his body forward, under the muzzle of the subgun, his head and right shoulder impacting the man's gut, the subgun discharging across his back, Frost driving the man backward, through the doorway, into the corridor, stumbling as a small explosion shook the floor beneath them, Frost's left fist knotted between the man's legs, the handful of testicles crushing in his fingers.

The soldier screamed as Frost's right fist slammed forward into the solar plexus, the subgun discharging again as Frost and the soldier fell to the carpeted floor, the smell here noxious, suffocating, nauseating.

He heard the clatter of the subgun, felt the right hand hammering—empty—at his neck and face. He reached with his left fist, the man screaming again, Frost rolling right, off the body, punching out with his right fist into the left side of the man's face, his knuckles coming back gilded black from the cammie makeup, and bleeding a little where bone had struck bone.

The soldier rolled, Frost unable to slip from under him, a knee smash coming at him, Frost feeling the hammering, then the sickness but taking most of it in his stomach rather than his crotch. Frost's right fist snaked up, punching into the Adam's apple, then punching into it again and again, the man above him coughing, choking, Frost's left hand moving down along the man's right leg. He'd seen it there—now he felt it, the hilt of a fighting knife strapped to the right calf. He tore at it, had it, then stabbed it laterally into the soldier's right side, withdrew, stabbed into the right kidney, withdrew, stabbed up and under the right armpit.

Screaming, cursing, the body sagged. The one-eyed man pushed the body away.

He rolled onto his stomach, coughing, gagging on the smoke, stumbling as he tried to push himself up, then clawed at the wall as he stood finally.

He dropped the bloodied knife, reaching down through the swirling smoke—the Sten. He had it. He felt the body—three spare magazines. He took them, staggering back as he rammed them into his belt.

There was gunfire—it would be the Flying Squad men in battle with more of the men like the three he had just killed.

He spat, his mouth dry, his throat burning.

He spat dry. Nothing.

Stumbling, he started running down the corridor—toward the sound of the gunfire.

Chapter Eighteen

Choking back the coughing spasm which had racked his body an instant earlier, Frost crouched as low to the floor as he could, the smell of the carpet better than the smell of the smoke. At the end of the corridor, beyond the corner behind which he hid, five of the Flying Squad men—perhaps all that remained, he thought bitterly—were pinned down, but in turn pinning down ten or a dozen of the black-clad, black cammie made-up soldiers.

Who were they? the one-eyed man wondered.

He knew faces now—remembered each face of the ones he had seen in the woods, had already realized that the three men he had killed were among these. Likely the ten or so at the end of the corridor were part of them as well. The hotel was a loss—escaping from it might prove impossible.

He had met death before—and if he died now, killing these men, there could be worse deaths. As if punctuating his thoughts, there was a small explosion, a section of the floor above caving in through the ceiling near the part of the corridor he had just left. The flames would be a worse death.

He changed to a fresh stick in the Sten gun, looking at his hands for a moment. They trembled slightly—not with the thought of his own death, but with the flood of memory the voice of the soldier he had fought and killed in the corridor had brought back to him.

O'Hara was very likely murdered, and Bess had been shot down before his eye.

The one-eyed man swallowed hard.

He peered around the corner, the gunfire louder now. It was like a ballet, a tragic ballet—you moved, the man you fought moved, one of you went down.

He smiled, whispering to his pounding heart, "Let the dance begin."

He was up, running, moving around the corner, his right eye streaming tears from the smoke, the Sten gun in his hands streaming gilding metal-jacketed 9mms toward the backs of the soldiers fighting the Flying Squad counterterrorist force, bodies pirouetting with the impacts, sailing across empty space as they crashed gracelessly down. The men turned toward him now, firing their submachine guns and assault rifles, the walls beside Frost ripping under the impact of their slugs, the men of the Flying Squad rushing the enemy position as Frost closed from their flank.

Five of the soldiers closed with Frost. Frost firing the Sten out, reaching to the falling body of a man near him, grappling a pistol from the tanker-style shoulder rig— mentally he knew it was a Beretta 92SB—and working the safety off, then double actioning the first shot, then another and another into the face of the man coming for him, the face exploding. The man fell against him, Frost losing the Sten gun but still firing the pistol. He felt something tug at his right side—a bullet, he guessed. He emptied the pistol into two more men charging at him, found a knife in the hand of another dead man and threw himself toward one of the soldiers, across the receiver of an FN FAL assault rifle, the gun crashing down, Frost ramming the knife home into the throat of the man holding it.

Frost picked up the assault rifle, began working the trigger, more soldiers coming down the corridor now, the Flying Squad men in the thick of the fighting.

One man down, then another and another and another—the FN FAL was empty.

A man lunged for Frost and missed, Frost looped the assault rifle's sling over his head, around the throat and stomped his right foot down between the shoulder blades, wrenching up and back on the rifle, the sling twisting the neck, breaking it.

Frost reached to the floor, taking the Sten gun from the dead man's hands, swinging the muzzle up on line, firing it out, the stick—empty—going to the smoking floor as Frost rammed one of the two remaining spares from his belt home and fired again.

Three of the Flying Squad men were still alive, one of them wounded; the soldiers in black were still coming. Frost pumped the trigger of the Sten. One man down. Another man down. A third man's head severed from the body as Frost swept the Sten's muzzle laterally left to right, the head rolling across the carpet. The Sten was empty. Frost, raking the butt of the subgun across another man's face, then hammering the butt down and forward as the body started to fall, crushed the nose and teeth, blood spraying at him.

He lost the Sten, something impacting his left side,

hammering him down.

Frost rolled with it—a man, a knife in the man's hands. The one-eyed man rammed his right knee up, rolling as the knife-wielding soldier rolled away.

Frost was up, on his feet. The knife wielder rushing him, Frost wheeled half-right, letting the man rush past; Frost's left foot doubled back kicking against the man's right side and right upper arm, the man falling against the far wall.

Frost wheeled right again, another one hundred eighty degrees. The man up, coming with the knife, Frost wrestling a knife from the sheath on the calf of a dead man at his feet, underhanding it across the width of the corridor into the exposed chest of the man with the knife. The man went down, Frost wheeling left, another attacker coming at him, Frost feigning a kick, side stepping, his right fist hammering up into the right temple of the man, killing him, the body tumbling, Frost dropping to his knees, grabbing up a Sten. Frost fired into the soldiers as they came. The Sten empty, Frost inserted the last magazine he had. He started firing again, men falling in front of him, spilling down.

The dance was over.

Two of the Flying Squad men stood, a third looking only half alive, lying bleeding against the wall.

Frost dropped the empty Sten, found a Colt Government Model .45 on the floor and jacked the slide, emptying out the chambered round. He left the hammer cocked, upped the safety and rammed the .45 into his trouser band. He shouted, coughing, his eye streaming tears. "Come on—let's get the hell out of here!" He started toward the injured Flying Squad member, shouldering the man up to a standing position, then bending his weight into the man's abdomen, getting the bleeding man up over his left shoulder.

Frost lurched forward, nearly falling, the man solidly over his left shoulder.

He drew the pistol from his belt with his other hand, his right fist clenched around it, his right thumb poised over the safety to drop it.

He walked, the other two Flying Squad men with FN FAL assault rifles flanking him. The corridor ahead was the only option, the smoke thick, heavy. The fourth floor—fifth in American parlance—led out onto a veranda. There was no hope of finding a safe way down.

The double glass doors to the veranda had been blown out. One of the Flying Squad men kicked away more of the glass, Frost stepped through. He suddenly felt light-headed, the rush of comparatively fresh air in the night filling his lungs.

The edge of the veranda—a railing. He stumbled toward it, sirens whining and screaming against his ears in the night.

One of the Flying Squad men was already at the railing, looking down. He shouted, "There are tall trees near us—we can make it over!" and then the man was slipping the railing. One instant he was at the edge of the veranda, the next leaping across air space as Frost sagged against the veranda railing.

He saw the whiteness of hands and face in the darkness of the tree, then there was an explosion from behind him, Frost closing his eye against it.

He opened his eye, the light on the veranda brilliant now. Frost looked back—the entire hotel was drowning in flames.

"Here, Captain Frost—hand over your man there!"

Frost nodded, coughing, the second Flying Squad man helping him to step over the railing under the weight of the injured man across his shoulder. Frost stood there, the second man crossing the railing, now helping Frost with the injured man.

The first Flying Squad man was extended on the furthermost reach of a broad limb, less than four feet from the veranda edge. Frost and the second Flying Squad member took the injured man in their arms, as if forming a chair, holding him as far out as they dared, Frost's arm aching.

The first Flying Squad member was reaching; Frost watched through his tearing eye as the man's left hand locked on the injured man's belt.

"I got Harry—one of you—over 'ere quick!"

Frost nodded, jumping for the limb, his left hand slipping, but his right holding the instant long enough to give him purchase, his left hand coming up.

Frost swung his right leg up, the limb shuddering as he straddled it. He skidded along its length to the first Flying Squad man, reaching down, getting a hand on the injured man's belt as well.

"Coming now," the second Flying Squad member shouted. He jumped. Frost lost sight of him, then heard the rustling of branches below him.

"Down here—let 'im down and I'll hold 'im—you fellas get help!"

Mechanically, Frost began lowering the injured man, the first Flying Squad member letting go first, then Frost shifting the burden.

Frost leaned back, balancing himself on the limb.

The first man looked back at him and grinned, saying, "Me—I love climbing trees, I do. What say I shinny on down and get a fire ladder and you just rest and relax a bit, Captain, and watch the fire?"

The one-eyed man laughed, nodded his head and closed his eye.

It still streamed tears—but the tears were no longer from the smoke. They were from the memories he wished had remained forgotten.

Chapter Nineteen

"The Argentine is the key—the key to it all," Thurmond said wearily.

Frost nodded, studying the gray light through Thurmond's office window. Both of them, after the destruction of the hotel in Kent, had slept the night in the office.

Frost's hair was wet still from the shower he'd taken, his face smoothed of the stubble—too much of it was gray these days, he thought—by a borrowed razor. The rest of his clothes—brought from the hotel—were in their suitcases at the far corner of Thurmond's office.

"Tell it all to me—you say you remember it all now."

Frost nodded again, lit a Camel in the flame of the Bic lighter and inhaled the smoke deep into his lungs. He smiled, thinking how stupid human beings were. He had his lungs filled with smoke. A medic had wanted him put under observation for smoke inhalation treatment, and he sat smoking a cigarette.

"Bess had become convinced that the murder-for-hire ring was being used, at least part of the time, for political assassinations. And efficiently—so efficiently that your typical killing didn't even attract any thorough investigation. But we were stonewalled. Then this report came across her desk—some school kids in a remote section of Northern England had been treated for a strange eye irritation. I think I told her it sounded like some kind of tear gas. We were all in Bess's and my room—O'Hara, too. We were eating room service that night. Mike agreed it was tear gas. Bess stood up—I remember just like I can see it," Frost sighed. "She stood up, took one of my cigarettes—never smoked anything but mine I think. She took one and told us that since we were all stonewalled on the murder-for-hire ring, why not take a day or two and investigate the thing with the kids and the eye irritation."

"And then what?" Thurmond asked, lighting a pipe with a single match—Frost hated people who could do that.

"Then," Frost nodded, biting his lower lip, then taking a drag on the cigarette. "Then Mike chimed in about renting a bigger car. Thinking about it now it probably didn't have a thing to do with his leg room—probably just wanted a car with a glove compartment big enough to hide his gun."

Thurmond laughed, and so did Frost for an instant. "Bess figured, she said, that if we went after this thing with the kids for a few days, well—well, maybe we could return to the murder-for-hire thing with a . . . she called it a 'fresh perspective.' Anyway, that's what we did. Rented the car and drove out to the area. Bess interviewed some of the kids and Mike used a map and pinpointed the most common spot where the kids seemed to first notice the eye irritation. It was sounding more and more like tear gas—one of the kids had broken blood vessels in his eyes from rubbing them, but his parents had said the doctors figured he'd be OK."

"Did anyone," Thurmond asked, "conjecture as to the source of the eye irritant?"

"Only Mike," Frost nodded, licking his lips. "Mike figured some British Army outfit had fouled up when it was on maneuvers or something and the government just hadn't leaked anything to the press."

"Here we rarely have to bother leaking anything to the press boys," Thurmond laughed. "They seem to make their own leaks, they do."

"Yeah—same in America," Frost smiled. "Bess now, well, she pegged it as some sort of industrial-related thing—maybe a chemical spill. So we all drove out there. Bess thought she saw something moving in the woods. That's when Mike stopped the car and took his Smith out of the glove compartment—said it was 'OK with the Limeys,' I remember that. He and Bess started into the woods first—I was walking behind them and hollering at O'Hara to tell me what the hell was going on if the British government had given him the OK to carry a gun. That's when I swatted my right cheek on that branch. Bess turned around when I swore or something, I guess, and she patted at the cut with her handkerchief. I heard O'Hara shout from up ahead—Bess and I started running after him. He hadn't stopped when Bess had and he'd gotten ahead of us. There was some kind of cloud—localized—and there was Mike, throwing up his breakfast all over the ground. I pushed Bess back, took a good breath of the clean air and ran into the clearing after Mike. I grabbed him, got him to his feet, then I grabbed his gun—I started hauling him out of there. I got him out of the cloud; my eye was tearing real bad by then. Bess

131

shouted something and I hauled Mike into the trees. O'Hara was still throwing up and my stomach was feeling kind of bad. There were soldiers—they'd seen Bess, I guess. They were running toward her. Had FN FALs, duty holsters with High Powers in 'em—the whole works. Some kind of commando outfit I'd figured. They were wearing gas masks—but not other decontamination gear. I started signalling to the guys that O'Hara was sick—I had his gun under my sportcoat, you know?"

Thurmond nodded.

"Anyway, some of the guys ran up to us. Then one of the guys from a little way back shouted through his mask that we should all be killed. He started to pull a pistol— must have been an officer—he wasn't carrying a rifle at all. He was shouting again—that the other guys should kill us. One of the soldiers raised his FN and was gonna shoot O'Hara or Bess, I don't know which. I pulled O'Hara's gun and shot the guy in the chest—almost broke my wrist doing it. Then—"

Frost stubbed out his cigarette.

"Then?" Thurmond asked, leaning forward, the pipe dead between his teeth.

"I guess—I guess somebody slugged me. I can't remember a thing, and it's not my memory this time. There just isn't anything there, ya know?"

Thurmond only nodded.

"But I remember waking up—kind of a cell. Bess was shot in the arm . . . I guess that's what I've been remembering. She was bleeding really bad—unconscious. O'Hara was trying to stop the bleeding between vomiting on the floor—just the dry heaves by then. But Bess I guess jumped between me and one of the guys with the FN FALs. That must be what I remember when I see her

132

getting shot."

"So, perhaps she's somehow alive—"

"She looked bad," Frost murmured. "Pale, sick—her chest was hardly rising. This medic—but a civilian guy—he came in with three guys in uniform. Brits, like the other guys. All three of them had FNs. The three guys took O'Hara and me outside. O'Hara tried fighting 'em—I was still groggy and my head hurt. Mike got a rifle butt in the nuts for it."

"Good God," Thurmond rasped.

Frost said nothing for a moment—he lit a cigarette. "I remember my cigarettes, my lighter, my watch, even my necktie and my belt were gone. All the guys outside had military uniforms on—I even remember the outfit patch."

"What was it?"

"No, not like that. I couldn't figure the unit, but if I saw it again I could."

Thurmond jotted something down on a note pad, then looked back into Frost's face. "What happened after you and O'Hara were brought outside?"

Frost closed his eye—he sighed long, hard. "I was helping Mike to walk and he was helping me. Wound up outside an old stone farmhouse or something—all these guys in military uniforms and in the middle of them a guy dressed in good casual clothes—expensive, real expensive looking. He was wearing a ski mask and gloves and he did most of the talking—maybe all of it. He told us we saw something we shouldn't have seen—and we were going to die for it."

Frost inhaled hard on the cigarette, standing up, walking toward the window. "He said he wanted to know everything we knew or we'd die real hard," Frost went on. "Real hard. Well, O'Hara, he was still having the dry heaves from the gas and he was doubled over from where the guy had whacked him in the crotch. But he stood up real straight and he shouted out—I remember it—he said, 'You're messing with the FBI here, punk—seventy-five years we been mopping the floor with assholes like you.' The guy in the ski mask said Bess had already been dealt with—they'd let her bleed to death—he had the medic standing beside him now. I shouted something and I don't remember what it was, but I jumped the guy nearest to me—my adrenalin was goin' I guess," Frost nodded. "Whacked him in the teeth with my right knee—couldn't get his gun though. O'Hara knifed a guy with his own bayonet—first time I think I ever saw Mike use a knife. You could tell Mike wasn't any good with one—left the thing stuck in the guy's rib cage 'cause he couldn't get it out. We both ran like hell into the trees—O'Hara got shot in the arm but kept running. We could hear the guys after us," Frost almost whispered, watching the early-morning London traffic through the window.

"Is that how you got away then?" Thurmond asked. "Well, lad?"

"No," Frost shook his head suddenly. "No," and he turned to look at Thurmond. "With Bess dead I wanted to take the guys out in the woods. Mike said we'd better split up and make a run for it—contact the cops. Double our chances of nailing the guys if we split. Maybe it was some kind of merc outfit or some terrorist thing, he said. I agreed—but I wanted to kill the guys that killed Bess. But I did what Mike said—we ran in separate directions. Last time I ever . . . ever saw Mike. He must be dead. They would have been caught by now if he'd made it in."

Thurmond only nodded.

"They caught me—cornered me near some cliffs—the one guy. The guy from before, the officer—not the one in the ski mask, but the guy—shit, he's the one who shot Bess there," Frost shouted, hammering his right fist against the wall. "When I shot that guy in the chest—couple of the other soldiers grabbed me. This guy—he picked up Mike's gun off the ground, aimed it right at my face, then Bess jumped at him between us and the gun went off and she hit the ground like a rag doll. That's when I got clipped in the head."

"So this same man," Thurmond urged, "cornered you again?"

"Yeah," Frost nodded, feeling cold sweat on his face. "Yeah—there were these cliffs and all of a sudden I was ringed by these guys. He had the gun—Mike's gun. He was even wearing Mike's shoulder holster by then. He leveled the gun at me. Then there was the guy in the ski mask—he said, 'Well, shoot the bloody bastard!' I remember that 'cause the words sounded muffled kind of through the ski mask. The man with Mike's gun, he looked at the guy in the ski mask—he turned back to me. I edged back toward the cliffs—I guess I figured I could jump for it. He shot—my head felt like it was being ripped off. I fell. I could still see—the rocks and everything coming up at me, the—the water," Frost concluded.

"What then, Captain, what then?"

"Not a . . . thing. Nothing real, maybe—I remember some hands and some faces—they were all like they were twisted out of shape. And there was a road and then I was driving someplace—I don't know. Next thing I really have any memory of was waking up in the alley in London before the fight with those guys."

135

"A lorry driver," Thurmond said, staring at the worn carpet. "Or perhaps a motorist. The first thing to do is splash your face across the newspapers—have you seen this man, that sort of thing. Find the driver who picked you up after you got out of the water—or perhaps some fishermen even pulled you out. God knows. But find someone who remembers you, match the geography to what you remember and we can find that house. We're starting for the wooded area immediately. I can arrange the helicopter flight out there," and Thurmond got up and moved to his desk.

He picked up the phone, but before speaking into it, his voice low, his left hand cupping over the mouthpiece, he whispered, "If justice can't get the men who killed Miss Stallman and Agent O'Hara—well, I'll give you your gun back and let you have the go at it yourself, lad. There's still honor, isn't there?"

He looked away from Frost and started talking into the telephone receiver.

Chapter Twenty

The flight to the woods had produced nothing—not an empty shell casing, not a cigarette butt that didn't belong—but Thurmond still had men combing the area. Even from the air, the house had not been visible. It was evidently someplace distant from the woods. Thurmond had ordered that everyone in the nearby hamlet be questioned about seeing military personnel, hearing shots—anything strange, peculiar or out of the ordinary. The helicopter on a concrete landing pad behind them now, Frost and Thurmond—the rotors whipping a cold wind that caused Frost to shiver under his brown leather bomber jacket—walked toward the three British Army officers waiting for them at the edge of the helipad.

Frost and Thurmond stopped, the officer in the center saluting, saying, "Inspector, Captain Frost—we're honored to be of assistance, gentlemen." He dropped the salute, saying, "If you'll both walk this way," and the man turned curtly on his heel and started off. He was bowlegged as he walked. Frost remembered the old vaudeville line, "Walk this way" but he passed it up and didn't mimic the man—he needed his help.

None of the standard unit insignia shown to him in the massive wall plaques was even remotely similar to the one he had seen worn on the shoulders of the commandoes in the woods—the ones who had murdered Bess, murdered O'Hara, nearly murdered him.

It was the officer who had greeted them—Maj. Darrien Blott—who suggested it finally. "Well, good God, man, why don't you take a scrap of paper and pen or something—then just draw it out for us, what?"

He sat in an office now, a cubicle, a blank piece of paper and a pen all that was on the desk, Thurmond and the others outside having coffee—Frost, alone, trying to remember the unit patch.

He closed his eye. He tried to see it—the patch, the skull that had been on it.

He picked up the pen.

It was a skull—a gaping mouthed, wide-eyed skull—but the eyes were only holes of blackness. He laughed at himself—he was a consummate non-artist. Then he stopped laughing, thinking that if he and Bess had someday had a child, even the least artistic child in the world could have outdrawn him. He continued, a flintlock rifle—it looked like a long, straight toothpick with a bump on it—and a saber crossed over the skull, the saber a curved toothpick with a "U" underneath it for the guard.

"Latin," he whispered, his Latin bad, rusty—but the motto had been something like "Legio Interiti." He wrote it down beneath the skull. "Endings are wrong maybe," he whispered to himself.

He stood up, walked to the office door and opened it, shouting down the hallway. "Inspector Thurmond, the men—the commandoes . . ."

Thurmond turned away from the British major and looked back down the corridor. "Yes?"

"The guys—they're the Legion of Death." The one-eyed man didn't know if the name meant anything to Thurmond—but when he said it again under his breath—"Legion of Death"—the words made Hank Frost shiver. . . .

They sat in the major's office, drinking coffee from china cups, Frost saying, "I only saw it once before—a long time ago. It was in Africa. A mercenary I was working with—an old guy. He'd worked for 'em all, at least according to the way he told it. Name was Vince something—I don't know if I ever knew the rest. He was in a sergeant's slot with the outfit. We were sitting around one night—all getting whacked in a bar in Rhodesia and he pulled this old patch out of his wallet and showed it to me—said he used to be a member. But he ran out on them, changed his name, shaved off his mustache and shaved his hair so he'd look different."

"I say," the major murmured. Thurmond said nothing.

Frost cleared his throat, sipped at the coffee—he was tired, very tired—and went on. "Old Vince said it was The Secret Army—the mercenary group you contacted for the ultimate clandestine operations, that it had been in business for more than a century, maybe a lot more than that. Allegiance to nobody—no cause, no politics. Killers—specialists in killing and killing—that's all. I had heard about the thing, but I figured it was just a spook story and that old Vince was rattled enough with the booze to think the old patch he had in his wallet was for real. Not that he was lying really. They killed a

139

reporter, an FBI agent—almost killed another mercenary," Frost told them. "Least that's what they call me sometimes—a mercenary."

"Say this—" Thurmond began.

"This," Frost smiled. "OK?"

"No—no, I'm serious—say that the Argentinean, say that he represented the people who hired this Legion of Death. That after all the attempts to kill you were botched—by the murder-for-hire syndicate, even some of the Legion of Death commandoes—say that the Argentine people who had hired both outfits, say that they sent in their own hit man. To kill you. When that didn't work, the Legion finally made a full military strike against you."

"All right, say that," Frost nodded.

"Legion of Death—my God—that's something out of a comic book, like a bad program on the telly!"

Frost looked at the major. "See how much you laugh when you lock horns with them. All of them take an oath to secrecy—according to old Vince. They all swear to die rather than be captured and reveal information about the organization—shit."

"There is no proof. We do have a way to go, though, lad," Thurmond said, looking at Frost.

"What? What way to go?"

"The things you told me about your time at that party with your lady friend."

"You mean the guy who was watching me? Maybe he—"

"Maybe he set the murder-for-hire people after you and the lady."

"Sir John Pinkham-Fletcher," Frost almost whispered.

"Perhaps he's the chap in the ski mask."

"Ski masks?" It was the major. Frost ignored him.

"We've been compiling evidence on the murder-for-hire syndicate," Thurmond began. "For some time, actually. And Agent O'Hara—I learned he was investigating the death of the American reporter your Bess had taken over for. Thought to be a tie-in with the American crime syndicate—and perhaps there is."

"You mean you had a suspect all this time and—"

"Suspect?" Thurmond smiled. "Hardly, laddie, just a few bits of circumstantial evidence—nothing more than him paying you some undue attention at that party, things like that. I understand the Yard has been watching him for months. He is suspected of murdering Monica Hewlett-Jones' husband, Jonathan. Sir Jonathan was working with the Yard trying to pursue politically motivated assassinations through some head man in the Foreign Office. He'd done some things for the crown before—what you might call espionage that we cannot talk about because of the Official Secrets Act and the like."

"I say," the major exclaimed.

"I say shut up," Frost told him, then grinned. Frost looked at Thurmond. "This Pinkham-Fletcher character, he's—"

"There's no evidence at all—but say he was hired by some Argentine faction that wanted some sort of revenge for the Falkland Islands affair. Let us say further that his murder-for-hire syndicate people couldn't handle it. Who better to find the Legion of Death, if it exists, than a past master at murder, what? Hey, laddie? But there's not a shred of hard evidence."

"These suckers in the Legion—I don't think they're just here in England practicing for the fun of it."

"Hmmm." Thurmond lit his pipe—again with one match. He turned to the major. "I'll need a telephone," and then he turned to Frost. "I'm ordering a raid on the estate of Sir John Pinkham-Fletcher. I'm also ordering your personal weapons released from bonded warehouse to you—I can do that. Not easily—but I can do both. And if," Thurmond smiled, "Pinkham-Fletcher is innocent— well, laddie, I hope you know some little town in the United States that could use an ex-British copper now."

Frost looked at the major. "Sorry I told you to shut up."

"But—"

Frost looked at the major again. "But—and what would you do, Major?"

The major stroked his mustache. "I'll contact my superiors. Perhaps the army might just be able to have an unexpected maneuver in the vicinity of Sir John Pinkham-Fletcher's estate, just perhaps."

The one-eyed man felt his face beginning to smile. He wanted the revenge—badly.

Chapter Twenty-One

Frost sat in the gray van, Thurmond beside him. Thurmond had a Remington 870 riot shotgun across his knees, looking incongruous with the dark overcoat and dark Homburg hat he wore.

Frost reached under his coat. His right fist grabbed at the black-checkered rubber-Pachmayr-gripped High Power—he snapped it free of the diagonal Cobra ComVest. He felt the weight in his hands, no need to check the chamber or the magazine—that already done. On his left ankle he wore Mike O'Hara's Smith & Wesson Model 60—maybe just for luck, he'd told himself. In the small of his back he had the little Gerber knife.

He reholstered the Metalifed 9mm High Power, then picked up the Interdynamics KG-99 9mm from the seat beside him.

"I feel woefully underarmed, lad," Thurmond laughed. "Just a Walther PP in my overcoat pocket and this shotgun."

"But you have the strength of ten 'cause your heart's pure," Frost told him.

"Aye—the strength of ten indeed, Captain Frost—the strength of ten indeed it is," and Thurmond laughed. The radio telephone beside Thurmond buzzed and Thurmond picked it up. "Thurmond here." There was a pause. "Aye—all of them then? Good. On my signal. And remember what our American friend has told us: the Legion—they die rather than surrender. Right," and Thurmond replaced the phone.

He looked past Frost, past the man beside Frost, toward the front of the van. "Arthur, drive us onto the Pinkham-Fletcher estate—we'll pay Sir John a social call as it were," and he handed the riot shotgun to the man across from him. Frost passed the KG-99 up to the man beside the driver.

"Wouldn't look good to go in there ready for a war, would it?" Frost nodded.

"Aye. But when he sees your pretty face, lad—well, if he's our man, then it's war there'll be, isn't it?"

The one-eyed man lit a cigarette—he always avoided giving obvious answers to rhetorical questions.

Chapter Twenty-Two

The door to the van slid open, Thurmond, standing up but still bent over as he walked to the edge of the van, looked out. Frost watched him intently—then stepped down onto the white gravel driveway.

Frost followed him out, unzipping the front of his brown leather bomber jacket so he could get to the High Power more quickly.

The one-eyed man had thought the Hewlett-Jones's "cottage" spectacular, but it was a veritable hovel, he realized, compared to the Pinkham-Fletcher estate. One of Thurmond's men had rewired the front gates to allow them inside without alerting the house. There was always the possibility, he realized, that if Pinkham-Fletcher were working with the Legion of Death, did run the murder-for-hire syndicate, that television monitoring equipment and other types of remote sensors were installed throughout the grounds. If that were the case, they would be expected.

Thurmond and one of the Flying Squad men started up the steps toward the double front doors, the building stretching side to side for at least two standard city blocks, Frost judged, and four floors high, of granite and brick mixed, the house appearing to have been built over a long period of years because of the mixed architecture.

Frost's right fist balled open and closed—he felt it, something about to happen.

Thurmond and the Flying Squad man were before the doors now, Thurmond knocking.

Frost didn't know what compelled him—perhaps his sixth sense was getting sharper—but his guts churned. He raced up the steps, snatching at the Metalifed High Power, diving toward Thurmond, shouting to the Flying Squad man, "Get out of the way!" Frost tackled Thurmond to the almost polished surface of the long porch, the door splintering as machinegun fire erupted, the one-eyed man rolling off Thurmond, firing his pistol in through the nearest window as he glanced right—the Flying Squad man was dead.

Thurmond was up, moving, surprisingly agile, Frost thought, for a man his age and build, the blued Walther PP in his right fist, his hat catching on the breeze and blowing away as he scrambled over the porch railing into the hedgerow. Frost was up, firing, flipping the railing right behind him. More machinegun fire and lighter, more spasmodic subgun fire from the house, windows shattering along the length of the front porch on both sides, assault rifle fire pouring down from the roof.

The PP in Thurmond's right fist fired once, twice, then a third time, Thurmond up and running for the van. Frost snatched at the Chiefs Special in O'Hara's Cobra ankle rig, the little Model 60 stainless in his left fist now, the High Power in his right, both guns firing as he climbed to his feet and ran from the hedges, the white gravel of the drive spraying up, pelting at him as he ran toward the van. It was already moving, Thurmond scrambling aboard, Frost still running for it.

Thurmond disappeared, then reappeared, firing the Remington 870 pump, another two men beside him in the open van door, crouched at its sides, firing FN FAL assault rifles. There was a ladder by the rear of the van, extending up to the chromed luggage rack. Frost stuffed the Model 60—emptied of its five shots—into his left hip pocket—he had no wallet—and poked the Browning into his trouser band. The van was picking up speed, Thurmond shouting over the roar of the gunfire, "Come on, lad, come on!"

Frost reached. He had the chest-level rungs of the ladder clamped in his fists; the van was picking up speed; his sixty-five-dollar-shoe-clad feet dragged across the gravel for an instant as the van lurched ahead.

He reached his right hand up, higher on the ladder rungs, pulling his feet up to the rear bumper. He found his High Power with the left fist, awkwardly, punching it outward toward the house, firing, bullets impacting the rear of the van then.

More gunfire from the van, the van hitting a curve in the driveway, the one-eyed man holding on tight.

Suddenly they were out of range, the van slowing down, stopping.

The one-eyed man stepped down from the bumper. He looked at his shoes. He hadn't really damaged them. He leaned back against the rear of the van, bending forward, holding the High Power in both hands between his legs, staring at the gravel driveway. Machinegun fire and assault rifle fire echoing across the grounds from around the bend in the driveway.

"Ya all right, lad?" Thurmond's voice came, beside him, Frost's eye closed now.

"Yeah," Frost rasped.

"You saved my life, Captain Frost."

Frost opened his eye, not raising his head but craning his neck to look at Thurmond.

"All police elements will be closing in—and the driver's contacting Major Blott. His unit will be coming up to support us. We'll nail the bastards, laddie."

Frost licked his lips, still trying to breathe. He looked up finally, seeing a clear view of the roof of the Pinkham-Fletcher manor house through the trees.

"Helicopter. Can't wait for D-day. We'll lose the men we really want and the rest of them will fight to the death. No, I need maybe a dozen guys—well armed. That greenhouse," and Frost pointed to the far side of the manor house on the right, glass panes glinting sunlight beyond the trees. "That greenhouse," he repeated. "Pelt a lot of heavy automatic weapons fire in there to prep the area, then we run in, fight our way into the main house. You get some snipers going to work on that rooftop helipad. As soon as the army gets here, let 'em try an envelopment from the two far left sides of the house—that'll draw off some of the heat we'll attract coming through the greenhouse."

"Ya lookin' to die, lad?" Thurmond asked him.

The one-eyed man, already changing sticks in the High Power, looked at Thurmond again. "Looking to kill, that's all."

He was looking to kill the Legion of Death leader—whoever he was—most of all, so much that he could taste it now.

Chapter Twenty-Three

He didn't believe thirteen was an unlucky number. Twelve SWAT-trained British policemen behind him, all heavily armed, Frost moved through the woods, far enough away from their edge that the harassing fire from the house was having no effect—except to make them keep their heads down.

He'd replenished the partially spent magazine for the High Power, all magazines—including the two twenty-round extension magazines, one of these loaded into the pistol now—fully charged. The High Power was under his jacket in the Cobra rig; the Interdynamics KG-99 was slung under his right arm, cross body, thirty-six-round magazine in place, the chamber loaded with a thirty-seventh round, the safety on. Two more spare magazines for the KG-99 were tucked inside his belt. In a borrowed musette bag he carried grenades—they looked like American war surplus fragmentation models. They probably were. Lend-lease was wonderful, he smiled.

He raised his left hand, signalling the twelve men behind him—all armed with Browning High Powers, FN

FAL assault rifles (7.62mm NATO) and some of the men additionally armed with Sten guns—to come to a halt.

He could see the greenhouse clearly now.

He nodded to the man nearest him, a police sergeant—about thirty, or younger. "Sergeant Chalmers, give the signal."

"Yes, sir," the younger man whispered. Then he talked into the radio. "Strike Force to Command Center. Strike Force to Command Center, are you reading me? Over."

It was Thurmond's voice coming back through the walkie-talkie. "Strike Force? Thurmond here. Ready for the fireworks? Over."

"Command Center, this is Strike Force. We are ready—repeating—we are ready. Strike Force out."

Sergeant Chalmers glanced toward Frost. Frost looked at him for an instant then looked beyond him to the other eleven men. The gunfire would be starting in a moment, gunfire to kill anyone inside the greenhouse.

Frost licked his lips. "The Legion of Death," he said loudly enough that he hoped they all heard. "If the stories are true, they're among the fiercest fighters in the world. They won't show you any quarter—don't show any to them. If it's a choice between killing one or wounding one, kill him. That maybe sounds brutal—well, maybe it is. But as long as that legionnaire is alive, he'll be trying to kill you or one of the other of us. So if you don't kill him, you may have one of your—we call it buddies, I think you use the word mates. Well, whatever—if you go easy, you may wind up with the death of one of your mates on your conscience. Or you may wind up dead yourself.

"The major and his military forces should be up in a

150

few minutes—once they are, we have to make it to the roof and stop that helicopter. The sniper fire Thurmond's been directing up there has been keeping them off the roof, but it hasn't hit the chopper as far as we can tell. We've gotta fight our way through the greenhouse, into the main house, then upstairs. By that time Major Blott's men should be closing in. Once these guys are cornered, two things will happen. The leaders will try to get out by helicopter, the rest of them will fight and die rather than surrender. I have no idea how many are in there—but we know they have assault rifles, heavy machineguns, subguns. Probably explosives. They have the defensive position—that's to their advantage. You guys are cops—policemen. They're professional soldiers. That's their edge, too." But Frost felt himself smile. "But we're the good guys, right? So that's our edge." The barrage was already starting on the greenhouse, the sound of glass shattering unmistakable as well. "So let's go and give 'em hell," he rasped. He pushed himself to his feet and started in a dead run out of the trees.

Chapter Twenty-Four

A frontal assault on the greenhouse was the only answer: the section of the greenhouse nearest the house under heavy assault rifle fire from Thurmond and his men, Frost leading his twelve police officers into the near side of the house to the doorway, glass in the roof and sides already shattered, Frost pumping a two-shot burst through the glass of the main door from the KG-99, the glass shattering, his foot kicking into it, knocking out the rest, then his left hand reaching inside, hitting the panic lock bar, Sergeant Chalmers beside him swinging the door open, both men dropping down beside the air-conditioning unit there as gunfire poured toward them.

"Chalmers," Frost shouted over the gunfire, the shattering of glass. "Get on the radio and have Thurmond stand by to pull off his covering fire so we can get in there."

"Right, sir," and Chalmers started to snatch at the belt pouch for the Motorola.

"Before that," Frost interrupted. "Take your best marksman—have him start shooting into the ceiling into

152

those sprayer nozzles that they use for watering the damn plants. I want that place flooded and quick—the water should come out with enough force to make it hard for them to stay under it and keep shooting at us."

"Right, sir," Chalmers nodded. The sergeant looked behind him. "Danner—front and center—on the double, Corporal!"

A blond-haired man—little more than a boy—crept forward, an FN FAL cradled in his hands like a baby. "Corporal, Captain Frost wants you to ventilate that sprinkler system in the ceiling. Get it watering the plants—looks a bit dry in there."

"Aye, Sergeant," Corporal Danner nodded, his eyes alight, almost laughing.

"Then hop to it, man!"

Without another word, Danner glanced left and right, apparently found the spot he wanted and then shouted, "Cover me, Sergeant!" He started across the open space beyond the air-conditioning unit, Frost ramming the KG-99 around the corner of the unit, pointing it blindly with his left hand, down the approximate center of the greenhouse, firing. Chalmers beside him, one hand still holding the door open, the other, holding a High Power, was firing as well. The others around them getting into it, firing.

Frost glanced left—Corporal Danner was in position.

"Cease fire," Frost shouted.

He reached down to the ground, finding a large rock beside him, propping it against the metal frame of the shot-out glass door.

"Thank you, sir," Chalmers nodded.

Frost watched Danner—the man settled into the rifle like most men would settle between the thighs of a

153

woman. It was a caress, not a hold. There was a single shot and Frost looked around the corner of the air-conditioning unit, hearing Chalmers warming up the radio. The first nozzle for the sprinkler system was gushing water now in a heavy spray.

Danner fired again—another nozzle started.

Frost made it that one, possibly two remained.

Another shot—another nozzle.

"There's one more, sir," Danner shouted. The young man fired, the fourth nozzle erupting.

Frost shouted to Chalmers, "Get that covering fire withdrawn—now," then he turned to the others behind him, "Follow me!"

The one-eyed man was up, running, through the doorway, glass shattering around him as gunfire seemed to pour from everywhere, potted plants bursting, exploding, wet dirt and plant debris flying everywhere, the water from overhead—icy cold seeming—pouring down in spraying torrents.

He kept running, pumping the KG-99 until the stick was dry, dropping the 9mm assault pistol on its sling, snatching for the Browning High Power, thumb cocking it, firing, firing again and again, Legion of Death soldiers in khaki battle jackets and black berets popping up everywhere at the far side of the greenhouse. FN FAL fire was behind him, around him, the police officers in his fighting unit crowding around him as they ran forward.

The enemy fire heavier now, the suppressing fire from Thurmond's element gone, Frost shouted, "Take cover," then dropped to the wet ground, slithering across the mud behind a wooden table loaded with geraniums.

He took the chance to change sticks on the KG-99, then shouted to his men, "Grenades—now!"

154

The one-eyed man snatched at one of the grenades from the musette bag, pulled the pin, holding down the handle, counting it off, then rolling it like a bowling ball down the center aisle of the massive greenhouse. He could see the blurs as other grenades rolled or sailed through the air.

He tucked down, covering his head and his eye with his leather-jacketed arms.

An explosion, then another and another and another, like a chain reaction, and as the explosives died, the sound of glass shattering everywhere.

"Watch out—she's gonna blow," somebody shouted, Frost looking up.

A large pipe across the ceiling. "Shit," and he shouted now. "Run for it—gas—natural gas!"

Frost was up, running, the police in front of him, all of them heading out of the greenhouse, the smell of the captan in the gas almost overpowering now.

There was a puffing sound, then a loud whoosh and Frost dove forward into the mud, through a shot-out section of glass, his shoulders snagging against the metal framework for the glass, his body going into a roll. As he rolled he saw it—a blanket of black-tinged yellow flame that covered the ceiling of the greenhouse, glass showering everywhere as he closed his eye, rolling his body through the mud away from the heat of the flames.

There were screams, curses, smaller explosions as Frost's body settled in a hedgerow.

He looked up. "Sergeant," he shouted.

"Captain Frost!" a voice called back.

"Chalmers—marshal the men, give me the casualties— we're going in." The flames were virtually dissipated, the twisted and gnarled framework of the greenhouse

155

steaming from the flames and the water that had drowned the greenhouse instants earlier.

Frost was up, inspecting his body—nothing broken, burned or badly bleeding. He felt a cut on the back of his neck, touched it, his hand coming away bloody. His left hand—the knuckles were scraped and bleeding. His right ankle hurt slightly as he put his weight on it, but it was a minor twist, he judged—a kink that would work itself out.

Chalmers's voice again. "Sir, one man down with a broken leg, two men with minor burns—they can still fight."

Frost could see him now, farther down the hedgerow beside what once was the greenhouse. "Leave the more seriously injured man with the burns with the one with the broken leg—they can give us some covering fire. Form on me," and Frost was moving, jumping the debris, out of the hedgerow, back under the creaking framework of the greenhouse, Chalmers, Danner, and the others coming. He started to run, toward the far side of the greenhouse, tripping, almost losing his footing over a charred and blackened body of one of the legionnaires. He kept running, no gunfire, no armed resistance now.

From the far side of the house he heard mortar fire—it would be Major Blott and his men, the legionnaires thus far not having exhibited mortar capability. Then more machinegun fire.

He kept running, nearing the edge of the greenhouse, the ground that had formed the floor muddy here, pieces of glass, pieces of human bodies, pieces of plants, and their containers—all of it littered everywhere.

Chalmers was up beside him, then Corporal Danner. Frost inhaled hard—beside him was a wooden door,

156

the glass in the upper portion shot or blown out.

Beyond the door would be the storage room for the greenhouse, he guessed, and beyond that the main house itself.

"All right," he sighed. "Probably some of them in there—maybe wounded. They'll fight Chalmers—take five men. Danner, you stick with me—standard fire and maneuver stuff like you guys had in your National Service periods, or at least some of you had. Chalmers, you handle fire for now, until Danner and I get into position—then the reverse, all the way through the house. Got it?"

"Yes, sir," Chalmers nodded.

"Let's move," Frost rasped, tapping four of the men on the shoulder. "You guys, you and you, too—you're with me. Come on," and Frost turned, drew up his right foot and kicked it out against the door at the knob, the door breaking outward, falling half off its hinges. He threw himself through, firing the KG-99 as fast as he could pull the trigger, Danner beside him, the FN FAL roaring fire.

Inside, there was nothing but burned-up dead men.

Chapter Twenty-Five

As they crossed from the service room into the main portion of the servants' quarters, there was no resistance—just a terrified butler and maid. Frost left one man to guard them just in case. They crossed into the main section of the house—a few of the Legion of Death men there, but more bodies of dead ones, mortars crashing through the far wing of the house, rubble and smoke and the dust from falling debris everywhere. Major Blott was personally leading a commando squad down the main hall, Frost linking with him, then calling up Chalmers and his men. Frost, Blott, Danner, Chalmers and two dozen military and police taking the stairs—broad, narrow-treaded, shallow stairs—three at a time in a run, the staircase leading up to a balcony that on each side fed into the second floor. Frost took his police to the right, Blott his commando force to the left.

Three more of the Legion of Death commandoes, a grenade attack, one of Frost's men going down with a chunk of either shrapnel or debris in his left arm that punched through into his chest—but the man was alive.

Frost ordered his men to counter with more grenades and they ran on.

On the far side of the building, farthest away from the gravel drive, they linked up again with Major Blott.

Frost, breathless, gasped, "They're leaving guys behind just to slow us up and keep us interested."

"Agreed," Blott nodded, red-faced from the run, Frost guessed. "I'll send six of my men along the next floor above to mop up—let's head for the roof, what?"

Frost nodded, changing sticks in the KG-99—it was his last. "Let's go," Frost rasped, starting for the back staircase, taking the steps in a run three at a time.

They hit the floor above, the six men Blott had chosen—one of them some kind of sergeant—breaking off on the clearing-up detail; Frost, Blott, Chalmers, Danner and the remainder of the force—more heavily police now—taking to the next flight up stairs, taking these two or three at a time as well.

They were nearing the top when Chalmers shouted, "Up there—legionnaires!"

Frost hurtled himself down flat along the stairs, rolling downward and to the right as the marble stairs took the impacts of submachine gun bursts, his own hands stabbing out as he impacted against the far railing, firing two-round, semi-automatic bursts with the KG-99, heavy assault rifle fire coming from the police and military with him, the men—a half dozen he could make out—at the head of the stairs withdrawing.

"Up—forward!" It was Major Blott shouting, Blott and his men—the police and Frost, too—now following, as Blott hit the top of the stairs, his High Power blazing as more subgunfire erupted from beyond the corner leading into the right-hand corridor.

Blott went down, spinning like a dancer on his toes, slamming against the wall, his hands dragging along it, blood tracing from his finger tips as the pistol fell to the floor.

"See to him," Frost shouted, leading the men toward the corridor, firing out the KG-99, letting the empty assault pistol drop to his right side on its sling, the Metalifed High Power with an extension magazine fitted up the butt in his right hand. He spotted one of the Legion of Death men, firing the pistol once, twice, a third time, the body spinning out, slapping against the wall. And then there was shooting everywhere, Frost closing with one of the legionnaires, firing three rounds from the High Power point-blank into the dark-featured face, the head seeming to explode, the left eye bulging out, bursting as the body slumped back.

It was Chalmers. "We're clean, sir!"

"The roof—watch it!" Frost started running, seeing a narrow staircase ahead at the far end of the corridor—it led upward, could only lead one place.

He hoped it didn't lead to failure and death, too.

Chapter Twenty-Six

At the top of the stairway leading to the roof was a solitary man with a submachine gun.

Frost shot him twice in the head.

What he saw on the roof, he saw in slow motion—no time to act.

Sir John Pinkham-Fletcher was standing beside the face of the man Frost recognized as the leader of the Legion troops, the man who had shot Bess, proclaimed she'd bled to death, the man who had pursued him, shot him in the head, the man who had launched the succession of attacks against him, the man responsible for the murder of Monica Hewlett-Jones.

The legionnaire leader had a riot shotgun—he raised it toward Sir John and the muzzle roared, Sir John's head dissolving in a pink liquid cloud of flesh and blood, the cloud caught up on the wind from the rotor blades of the chopper, Frost feeling droplets of the grisly moisture pelting his face.

A hand grenade in the legionnaire's left hand—tossed. Rolling. A stack of crates. The crates were labeled, Explosives.

The legionnaire leader was boarding the chopper, Frost and the others around him firing, then suddenly, Frost shouting, "The building's gonna go—jump for it! Jump! Now!" Frost, the men around him—all of them—ran for the edge of the roof, the hedgerow floors below them, grassy.

Frost's stomach churned. He was going to die—he jumped, throwing the KG-99 away from him as he did, FN FAL assault rifles littering the air as the others jumped around him.

Falling—weightlessness, his stomach churning, the ground rushing up to meet him. A roar from behind him—it was the building blowing, he realized. The ground, his eye focusing on a single leaf in the large hedge he was falling toward, watching the leaf, his hands going out to protect his face, the leaf huge now and . . .

Chapter Twenty-Seven

His head ached and he opened his eye and his head ached more.

"Captain—laddie—are you with us, man!"

Frost opened his eye. "Hey, Inspector, I gotta be dead so let me alone, huh?" Frost closed his eye again, then realized the logical absurdity. If he was dead Thurmond wouldn't be talking to him. Thurmond wasn't the type—unless, of course, Thurmond was dead. But Thurmond hadn't looked dead.

And Thurmond hadn't been in the building either.

So he shouldn't be dead.

Frost decided to open his eye again.

"What do you want, Inspector?"

"Wanted to see if you were still among the living—and you are, don't try to move. Medic will be here in a flash," and then Thurmond looked away, shouting, "Medic! Treat this man!"

"Hey," Frost whispered. "Don't shout, huh—my head." Frost sat up.

His back was stiff and as he placed his palms under

him, his palms got all squishy and wet. "Gee whiz, I musta—"

"It's the mud," Thurmond said, crouching down in it, propping Frost up. "You shouldn't be movin', laddie."

"Hey, look, I'm cool, huh," Frost nodded. And his neck hurt.

He wiggled his toes inside his sixty-five-dollar shoes— he noticed that his whole body seemed to be covered with mud. That was odd. He closed his eye. He figured he was fainting. . . .

Chapter Twenty-Eight

The one-eyed man sat on the edge of the door frame for one of the vans—his headache reasonably well gone, every bone in his body reminding him it was there but not really hurting. He was stiff, and he stood up, stretching, to walk near the van. He took up the styrofoam cup with the hot black coffee laced with bourbon and sipped at it, squinting his eye against the taste and the sunlight.

He looked up at the sky, away from the sun, toward the patterns of billowing clouds, then murmured, "Thanks, God," and nodded his head. That he was alive, had no broken bones, not even a compression fracture was not a minor miracle—it was a full-blown, one hundred percent act of God, he had decided. When the greenhouse had exploded, the water main feeding the sprinkler system had ruptured, flooding the ditch dug on the house side of the hedgerow to provide a new sewer line. The ditch was eight feet deep. The main, bursting, had filled the ditch, muddying the sides. When he'd jumped from the roof to evade the effect of the explosion, he'd crashed down into the hedgerow and skidded along the muddy side of the ditch and into the ditch itself, then down into the water. The mud at the bottom—soft—had prevented him from breaking every bone in his body, and Thurmond—mud-covered himself—had waded down into the ditch and pulled him out before he'd drowned.

Five other men from the roof were dead, among them Chalmers, the sergeant. Corporal Danner was en route to a hospital with his left leg broken in possibly three places and the fingers of his left hand broken. Danner, before they'd carted him off, had smiled, telling Frost and Thurmond, "Well, at least my gun hand is all right for shooting." And it was. Major Blott had never made it out of the building after being wounded, three more men—his—were unaccounted for and presumed dead somewhere in the still-burning rubble, as was Blott himself.

Sir John Pinkham-Fletcher was dead—shotgunned. And the leader of the Legion of Death commandoes was gone, by helicopter.

The number of legionnaires killed was estimated at twenty-five. More bodies might be discovered in the house.

Frost set down his styrofoam cup and lit a Camel.

He had to think.

Why had so many of the Legion of Death members been at the Pinkham-Fletcher estate—and why the presence of the leader there?

He shook his head. Perhaps it was the fall—he couldn't think.

"Captain Frost?"

Frost turned and looked behind him, toward the sound of the voice. It was Inspector Thurmond. "Yes?"

"The first of the newspapers out netted us a lorry driver," Thurmond began, stopping, standing in front of Frost, hands on his hips over his mud-soaked overcoat. "The man picked you up on a ride south to London. He was a bit reluctant to come forward because picking up a

166

hitchhiker was against his company policy and insurance regs—but he came forward anyway. A good man—Scotsman, of course."

Frost felt himself smile.

"We blanketed the area while all this was going on. Found the house where you, Agent O'Hara and Miss Stallman were held prisoner. No bodies, but some empty shell casings—some .44 Magnum casings, as a matter of fact. While we were en route here, the Yard and some chaps from S.I.S. were visiting Pinkham-Fletcher's offices at the Foreign Office. Nothing. His assistant wouldn't talk or didn't know anything—possibly both."

"Then it's a dead end. We'll never know what the Argentines—"

"Not quite," but Thurmond didn't smile. "When the house was discovered," and Thurmond walked over beside the van, seating himself on the edge of the door frame. "When it was discovered—the house where you and the others were held, that is—a forensic team was sent in, naturally."

Frost inhaled hard on the cigarette. "And?"

"No other woman has figured to be involved with these legionnaires, correct?"

"Right. Just Bess—what—"

"Had she, ahh," and Thurmond looked down at the ground, appearing to study his muddy shoes, "ahh, was it her time of the month when she was taken prisoner?"

"No, her period wasn't due for a couple of days yet."

"Then she may be alive," Thurmond said, looking up.

Frost dropped his cigarette.

"Standard procedure when a house is being given the full treatment is to pull the traps from all the plumbing to see if any evidence might have been washed down a drain. You and Miss Stallman slept together, correct?"

167

"Yeah," Frost nodded, for some reason feeling defensive.

Thurmond bit at the second knuckle of his right fist for an instant. "In one of the traps—there was a clog. Nasty stuff to go through. But they found evidence of a woman having a period. Did she use the sort that can be—"

"Yes, I think so—yeah."

"Did she carry some in her handbag as women sometimes do—with her menstrual period approaching?"

"Yeah, she always carried a couple."

"She was alive then—after the time they said she was allowed to bleed to death. If your reckoning is right, and the trauma of wounding didn't effect the onset of her cycle, she was alive for at least several days afterward."

"And she could be alive—"

"Now. Yes. She could be. I'm wagering that the helicopter that got away is going to their headquarters—not the house, not here. I'm wagering whatever their operation was that they planned a go at it soon—the forces held here were a reserve, just in case. Some strike at England's heart."

"How the hell do we find their base?"

"Our only hope is Pinkham-Fletcher's assistant at the Foreign Office. He's being brought here. If he did lie and knew his master's plans, then there's a chance. Perhaps even a chance your Miss Stallman is alive still. Though why they might have kept her alive I can't fathom actually. What I'm telling you, lad," and Thurmond stood up. "The butler you captured and the maid—they don't know a thing. This assistant to Pinkham-Fletcher, he may know. I canno' force him to talk. But I can arrange things for yoú to have a few moments alone with him—do you get my meaning, lad?"

The one-eyed man closed his eye. "Yes."

168

Chapter Twenty-Nine

His name was Richard Bell—and happily, for Frost, he wasn't that small a man. He was an inch or so taller than the one-eyed man, slender build, long armed, with dark, thinning hair.

They stood—alone—in a clearing in the woods fronting the smoldering wreckage of the Pinkham-Fletcher manor house.

Frost was unarmed. His clothes still covered with mud, the bomber jacket left back at the van along with his weapons. He had no idea what Thurmond had told the other police, military and now S.I.S. officials near the vans, other than that he—Frost—might have success in questioning Bell that they had not.

Bell stood, feet spread apart.

Frost spoke, "I want to know everything you know about Sir John Pinkham-Fletcher's association with the Legion of Death, with the Argentines, everything."

"I don't know a bloody thing—I told that to the authorities. And I demand my rights. What the bloody hell am I doing here?" His voice was slightly nasal, and

169

Frost noticed the nose. It had been broken at least once.

"You box?"

"I did in school, yes."

"Keep it up?"

"Yes, good way to stay fit."

"I agree," Frost told him. "See, these Legion of Death guys. Maybe murdered my woman, probably murdered my best friend, murdered another woman who helped me, tried murdering me a whole bunch of times. They're here for a reason—here in England. If you don't know anything, I'll apologize up front. But I'm going to beat the shit out of you until you talk or I'm satisfied you really don't know anything."

"Don't be absurd," Bell murmured disdainfully. "I know my legal rights."

"Good for you," Frost smiled. "You wanna talk, or get the crap kicked out of you?"

"You'll find yourself in prison over this."

"I don't care," Frost smiled. "I don't have much time though—so what's it going to be?"

"Bloody Americans—watch one too many John Wayne films and you think you can fight anyone."

"Right on," Frost smiled.

"I won't fight you."

"Just makes it easier for me," Frost answered.

The one-eyed man started walking, closing in on Bell. Bell edged back a few paces, stopping, then standing his ground. Frost stopped. The one-eyed man feigned with his left, smashing his right arm forward, his right fist clipping Bell in the right cheek. Bell stumbled back.

"This is barbaric," Bell gasped.

Frost shrugged. "So's the Legion of Death." Frost crossed Bell's jaw with his left, hammering Bell down to his knees.

"You—" and Bell looked up. "You can't honestly intend to keep hitting me until—"

Frost kicked with his right foot, hitting Bell's right arm, the arm propping him up, Bell lurching back to the ground. "Yes, I do," Frost smiled. "Why don't you defend yourself? I won't feel so bad, then."

Frost stepped back, Bell getting to his feet. "You can't—"

"I want to find out if Bess Stallman is alive. If she is, I wanna get her out from wherever she is—alive. If she isn't, I wanna kill the bastards who did it. Either way, I need to find the Legion of Death."

Bell swung with his left, Frost instinctively blocked it; the right followed through, Frost snapping his head back, Bell's fist missed him by less than an inch. Bell's left— Frost ducked it, hammering out his own left into Bell's abdomen, then a right to the face, then a left to the gut again, then a right into the chest, then a left and a right across the jaw, Bell falling back.

Bell's mouth was bleeding.

Bell threw himself forward, fists hammering out, Frost taking a halfhearted shot in the jaw, countering with a left to the solar plexus, doubling Bell forward, then a right uppercut to the tip of Bell's jaw, snapping him back, flipping him away and to the ground.

Frost stepped back, rubbing his knuckles—they were skinned and bleeding.

"I know—I know nothing," Bell insisted, spitting teeth, blood dribbling from the right corner of his mouth.

"Fine," Frost nodded, a little out of breath. "After we do this for a while longer and I'm really convinced, I'll get Thurmond to put the word out on the street that you spilled your guts about the Legion, about the murder-for-hire syndicate—everything. If you really don't know anything, the Legion and the syndicate won't have any reason to nail you. But if you do—"

Bell pushed himself to his feet, throwing himself forward, catching Frost on the left side, throwing off the one-eyed man's balance, Frost rolling away, Bell on top of him, Bell's fists hammering down toward Frost's face, Frost punching into Bell's rib cage, Bell twisting away, Frost's left elbow free—a fast snap to the mouth, Bell screaming, falling away.

Frost was up, his right foot snapping out, the toe of his sixty-five-dollar shoe impacting against Bell's testicles.

Bell screamed, Frost reaching down, hauling Bell up, a short shot to the gut, then another and another, Bell falling, Frost holding him up, his left hand knotted into Bell's shirt front, his right, open palmed, slapping Bell across the face, palming him, backhanding him, blood spraying from Bell's lips and nose now, Bell screaming through it, "Wait—Christ, wait!"

Frost let go of Bell, let him sink to his knees in the grass.

Looking down at him, the one-eyed man snarled, "You do know. You do know."

Bell looked up, then let his head sag. "Won't do you any bloody good. The girl's alive—or at least they planned to keep her alive. And so's the other American—the policeman. But it won't do you any damned good."

Frost, his voice barely audible even to himself—strange sounding, colder, more deadly sounding than he'd ever heard it—asked, "Why?"

"They're gonna kill 'em—leave their bodies there to implicate the Americans as being involved. They weren't gonna kill you and the other man. They wanted to leave you there most of all—the most damning thing. An American mercenary."

"What is it they're doing?" Frost whispered.

Bell raised his left arm, Frost taking a half step back. But Bell was only looking at his wrist watch. And then Bell laughed. "In just about fifteen minutes they're invading Windsor Castle to murder the royal family."

Frost wheeled right, the toe of his left foot catching Bell in the jaw, knocking him out.

And then the one-eyed man was running.

Chapter Thirty

It was the stuff nightmares were made of, Frost thought. With Lieutenant Crisp, ADC to the late Major Blott, Inspector Thurmond and a helicopter pilot, they moved in the Bell Long Ranger III past Heathrow Airport, toward Windsor Castle. All communications with the castle were cut off—something wrong with the telephone lines. The local police post couldn't be contacted either. Thurmond had patched through to a local police radio car and learned that a long column of military trucks had turned off M4 five minutes earlier— it put them, according to Thurmond, approximately ten minutes away from Windsor Castle. The only military unit anywhere near the area that could move into action quickly enough was the remnants of Blott's force from the attack on the Pinkham-Fletcher estate. Thurmond had gotten hold of a BBC executive and had him promise to immediately begin broadcasting on both television and radio that Windsor Castle was under attack, that telephone lines were down and that the royal family should evacuate.

Thurmond had confided that there was almost always at least one helicopter there—when the royal family was present, both Prince Philip and Prince Charles being competent helicopter pilots. If the BBC messages worked—a slim chance at best—and were believed, either the queen's husband or son—the future king— could fly key members of the royal family to safety.

It would take Blott's residual force, under the command now of a Captain Strickland, at least twenty more minutes to reach Windsor Castle, and that "driving like blazes" as Thurmond had put it.

So for the critical first ten minutes of the assault by the military convoy—the Legion of Death disguised as British Army regulars—it would rest solely with Thurmond, Lieutenant Crisp, the helicopter pilot—a policeman—and Frost.

At the pilot's best estimate, they would arrive the same instant the Legion trucks pulled inside through King George IV Gateway of the Long Walk, a road leading between the castle and the royal chapel in Windsor Great Park. "Thank God for the Thames," Thurmond had said—it blocked the most direct route into Windsor Castle grounds from the side of M4, the major artery passing nearest the Castle grounds.

If a member of the royal family, or someone on the staff, heard the BBC announcements, it would make it that much easier for the Legion to penetrate the grounds—they would be expected as the rescue column, for they wore British uniforms.

Entering by George IV Gateway from the south, a mere short turn to the right would lead the Legion into the royal family's private apartments.

Thurmond had outlined all of this over the intercom

radio as the helicopter had sped toward Windsor.

Frost had, in turn, been checking the FN FAL rifles, the Stens, and his own personal weapons. He was still caked with mud, his weapons had been watered heavily, but would work until he had time to clean and lubricate them. The mud was already starting to cake and fleck off his sixty-five-dollar shoes.

Frost took Thurmond's wrist and looked at his watch. "Landing in two minutes," he told him.

"Right."

"You know like the good guy always says in the movies—"

"What?"

"I've got a plan. Can the pilot hear me?"

"Loud and clear, sir," the policeman piloting the Bell answered, glancing back at Frost.

Frost nodded, saying, "This thing got a PA speaker?"

"Yes, sir."

"Good—there's a town near Windsor?"

Thurmond: "To the north, the west and a little to the south—yes. Why?"

"Inspector Thurmond gets hooked up to the PA system, we overfly the town. Everyone loves the queen, right?"

"She's everything that's England, sir," the pilot answered.

"Good, let's get everybody in that town out and rushing the Castle—we don't need troops with assault rifles. We've got maybe a couple hundred people with shovels and butcher knives and everything else you can kill with that can help us."

Thurmond looked at Frost. "Genius," Thurmond whispered through the radio.

The one-eyed man hoped so.

176

Frost could hear it on the PA through his own headset. "A group of international mercenaries is en route along the Long Walk to George IV Gate, their intent to kill all members of the royal family—the queen, Prince Philip, Prince Charles—all members. From our vantage point, their convoy can be seen coming toward the Gate now. This is the reason why your telephone communications are undone. Turn to the BBC—they will confirm the attack is about to take place. Rise up—pick up what weapons you can. We fight to save the queen!"

Frost felt something in his throat—emotion. It was good to think of people en masse loving that way. For in the streets below, cars stopped, people were running. A woman carrying something that from the distance could have been a meat cleaver, a bowler-hatted man brandishing a furled umbrella.

They had crossed to parallel the Henry IV Gateway, the last of the military convoy of the Legion of Death entering through the gateway from the Long Walk, past the wrought-iron fence with its two little light posts and flanking sentry houses. The sentries were looking up, Thurmond on the PA system again. "This is Inspector Thurmond of Scotland Yard. Stop those trucks—they're not our men, they're mercenaries out to slaughter the royal family."

One of the sentries moved into action, a burst of gunfire coming from the nearest truck—the man went down. Frost rasped into his headset microphone, "Overfly that truck—now!" It was the last truck and the helicopter banked steeply then dropped down, Frost barking into the microphone, "Hold over that truck until I jump onto the top!"

"You'll be killed for sure, lad," Thurmond snapped.

"You and the lieutenant—or 'leftenant' or whatever

you say—keep shooting down into those trucks—not the one I'm on. See ya," and Frost undid his seat belt, slinging one of the FN FALs cross-body under his right arm, the assault rifle bumping into the KG-99, spare mags for the FN rifle in the musette bag along with grenades.

He forced open the port-side passenger doorway, climbing down against the wind of the slipstream onto the runner, the military truck immediately below him.

With his left hand he reached to the small of his back, finding the butt of the little Gerber boot knife, unsnapping the thumbreak, holding the knife in his left fist.

The helicopter seemed almost about to stall, matching speed with the slow-moving truck below.

Frost took a last glance at Thurmond, shot his old friend a wink and jumped.

His midsection impacted against one of the canopy ribs and all the air in his lungs came out in a rush, the spearpoint of the Gerber digging in through the canvas, anchoring him as the truck swayed below him.

He snatched the knife and pushed himself to his feet, lurching forward toward the roof of the cab, automatic weapons fire coming from the truck bed under the canopy where his body had just been as he sprawled onto the truck cab.

The truck was picking up speed, but gunfire from the helicopter was raining down now, cutting a barrier into the bleached concrete road surface, blocking it, the one-eyed man putting the knife into his teeth.

He swung the FN FAL behind his back, reaching instead for the shorter, more maneuverable KG-99. He popped the safety, then rammed the KG-99 over the right side of the cab—to get the driver. He started pumping the trigger, pumping, trying to empty the thirty-six-round magazine. The truck started swerving now—he couldn't tell if he'd gotten the driver and his mate or if the driver was just trying to shake him.

But the truck was slowing again as the automatic weapon fire from the helicopter increased. The KG-99 was empty now and Frost pulled his gun back up, shifting it across his back.

"What the hell," he rasped, edging across the cab roof, then peering down from the left side—both men in the cab were dead or the next best thing to it.

He didn't smile—death was business, not pleasure.

He swung his legs around, clawing at the rain gutter over the windshield, trying for a handhold, finding just enough, letting his legs down, getting a foothold on the truck's running board.

The window was wide open, the one-eyed man reached across the windshield—the truck was veering off into the trees to the left. He hauled up against the windshield, pried open the door from the inside handle and let the door swing out. First his right hand, then his left grabbing at the window frame, he let his body swing out, again getting his feet onto the running board.

He was inside, shouts coming from behind him in the truck bed, something that sounded like a fight.

He shoved the body of the driver's helper out to the ground, sliding across the seat, raising his legs to get them over the floor-mounted stick, then shoved open the driver's side door, pushing the driver out to the ground.

He had the wheel in his hands, cutting it sharply to the right, back onto the road.

His left hand reached up to the knife, snatching it from his teeth, holstering it awkwardly.

There was a truck immediately ahead of him, perhaps twenty-five yards away—and the gunfire from the helicopter had stopped, the helicopter speeding over into the Castle grounds now. Frost found the gear pattern, shifting up into third then, when there wasn't any power, double clutching down into second. He wanted the next truck. His own vehicle was picking up speed, Frost crowding the right-hand door to keep as far out of range as possible of gunfire from the back of the truck. There was gunfire aplenty now, but the fight seemed to be inside the truck bed itself, not directed at him, not directed outside the truck bed at all.

"O'Hara," Frost shouted. "O'Hara!"

He heard the voice—muted because of the canopy, the gunfire. "Frost! Shit—come and help me!"

The one-eyed man stomped the brake pedal, wrenching the emergency on, throwing himself in a lurching run out of the truck, running its length, reaching the rear of the truck bed, flipping back the canvas there—there was a brawl, gunfire erupting from automatic weapons, through the opening now as Frost ducked down. He threw the FN FAL into an assault position at his right hip, spraying on full auto to the far left of the truck, O'Hara—dressed as one of the Legion commandoes—locked in hand-to-hand combat with two men in the far right rear of the truck.

Three of the legionnaires went down, then two more, Frost tucking back, dropping the empty magazine, ramming a fresh one home from the musette bag, then firing it out, O'Hara hurling one of the two men he grappled with into the path of Frost's gunfire, Frost killing the man. Frost edged back—no movement in the truck except O'Hara and the one man he still fought. Then O'Hara's left moved, fast, the man dodging, O'Hara's right hammering in, followed up with a knee smash into the crotch, the man doubling over, O'Hara snapping a classic karate chop across the back of the

180

man's neck—once, twice, then a third time, the body tumbling forward.

The tall, lean—leaner than when Frost had seen him last—FBI agent turned to him and smiled. "Told Bess and me they killed ya—I kept tellin' her they hadn't."

"She is alive—" Frost stammered.

""Up in the first truck there with the asshole that runs this operation—Robert Walter, calls himself a colonel. I think he's a pile of dogshit."

Frost felt his face smile. "Robert Walter—I'm gonna kill him."

"You gotta stand in line. He's wearin' your watch, lighting his smokes with your lighter, carrying my 29—" and then O'Hara's voice dropped. "He took Bess. I put up a fight, ya know—but there were six of 'em and I was still workin' on a number two and three when they hauled her out. He was gonna rape her—but she got him. She was havin' her period. I remember Bess laughing afterward. She thought she'd never be happy having her period when she was miles away from civilization, didn't have any, well, you know, nothin' left—but she just laughed. Walter just got up and left her."

Frost reached down to his ankle, unstrapping the Cobra rig there, handing it up into the truck. "Figured you might like this—I used it a little. Hope you don't mind."

"You kill some of these bastards with it?"

"Yeah, tried at least," Frost told him.

Then the one-eyed man started moving, running toward the front of the truck. "Get all the guns and stuff you think we can use—come up forward fast—we got a war to catch!"

Robert Walter. Frost was going to kill him.

181

Chapter Thirty-One

Already, as they drove through the Henry IV Gateway into the Castle grounds proper, in the side-view mirror Frost could see the townspeople coming—hundreds of them: men, women, carrying sticks and rocks and clubs. In their forefront, he could see an old man, and on the man's head was what looked like a World War II air raid warden's helmet.

Beside the one-eyed man, O'Hara was stripping away the uniform blouse with the Legion of Death patch on the sleeve. "Don't wanna get myself shot by a friendly."

"Little danger of that," Frost told him, cutting the wheel hard right after the trucks. "Aren't too many of us friendlies around."

"Here, put one of these on—that gas they used on us before, they're gonna use it again. Here—the stuff's bad."

"I know, I remember watching you."

"They were plannin' to kill me and kill Bess during the fight—leave us here, set it up so there'd be two Americans found dead here, working with the Legion of

182

Death to kill the royal family. That way the Argentineans—"

"Argentines, I think you say."

"Whatever the hell—but the Argentineans would get back at England for the Falklands thing and get back at America for helping England—rotten bastards."

"Remember Inspector Thurmond?"

"Yeah."

"I been workin' with him on this," Frost shouted, the engine roaring as he downshifted, "and he figures just a group of Argentine crackpots maybe—not an official government action."

"Makes sense," and Frost looked at O'Hara, O'Hara's voice strangely muffled. The gas mask was in place.

As Frost braked the truck, he pulled the gas mask on that O'Hara had given him, popping the cheeks to seal it as he blew through the filter. Already, his face felt like it was inside an oven.

He threw open the driver's side door—the battle was begun.

A Legion mercenary looked back at him. Frost shot the man's face away with a burst from the FN FAL—Fusil Automatique Legere. It was war.

Gas clouds were billowing across the grassy courtyard between the walled structure to Frost's immediate right and a central, circular tower—he imagined it had been built as the place for the last-ditch stand in the days when castles were fighting forts instead of royal residences. The few castle defenders were dropping, some of them vomiting as they fell, the strange gas—powerful, an eye irritant, and producing nausea—doing its work.

The one-eyed man started to run toward the nearest knot of the legionnaires, O'Hara shouting from behind him, "Walter will wanna get Bess as near to the royal family as possible before he drops her."

Frost remembered Thurmond's description of the Castle—to his immediate right was the entrance to the royal family's private apartments. The one-eyed man started for it.

A half-dozen of the gas-masked legionnaires dead ahead—Frost threw himself down beside a low stone block, firing the FN, O'Hara beside him in the next instant, shouts and screams coming now as the townspeople raced into the courtyard, the first wave overcome by the gas—but the one-eyed man smiled. The old man with the air raid warden's helmet was still on his feet— the gas mask he wore looked like it was World War I surplus. The one-eyed man laughed, then turned to face the legionnaires, O'Hara beside him, both FN FALs spitting fire, Frost shouting through the mask, "Come on— we rush 'em!" And he was up, running, O'Hara beside him, the one-eyed man jumping the body of a fallen guard, running toward the entrance into the Castle, the legionnaires firing, Frost firing, O'Hara firing, the one-eyed man feeling the air ping around him, the legionnaires going down.

Frost hit the doorway, went inside fast, firing, the stick empty, the KG-99 coming up, the assault pistol belching two-round, semi-automatic bursts at the legionnaires in the long, red-carpeted corridor to his left.

One man down, then another and another, the one-eyed man's left leg going from under him, his thigh burning, screaming to him. He stumbled, forward, still firing.

O'Hara was on his knees beside him, the FN FAL spitting death. More legionnaires dropped, the one-eyed man

184

reaching into the musette bag, finding a grenade.

He pulled the pin, counted it out, and lobbed it forward down the corridor, shouting to O'Hara, "Mike—down!"

Frost threw himself back, covering his head with his hands, the sound of the explosion magnified as it reverberated off the stone walls of the corridor.

Frost rolled onto his back, changing sticks for the FN FAL—seven legionnaire bodies littered the corridor, as did pieces of suits of armor, medieval weapons, chunks of plaster and pieces of furniture.

"Help me up, damnit," Frost snarled, O'Hara bending to him, the FBI agent's left shoulder crimson over the khaki shirt with fresh blood.

On his feet, Frost looked at his friend. "You walkin'?"

"Hell, no—I'm runnin', but I gotta wait for you and the gimp leg ya got now!"

The one-eyed man laughed, lurching forward, hugging along the wall to support himself, the FN FAL held ahead of him like a wand.

There was a knight's lance on the floor, broken by the force of the explosion. Frost picked up a three foot section of the tapered business end, holding it in his left hand, shifting away from the wall, limping on it like a cane.

He moved ahead.

They reached the end of the corridor, a fresh gas cloud there.

"That must be where the royal family is," Frost heard O'Hara rasp through the mask.

"Yeah," Frost nodded.

There would be the top of the Legion there, the cream of Walter's fighting men—and Robert Walter himself. And Bess. And the royal family of England.

Frost started along the small corridor—a child's toy in the center. He stepped over it. A toy truck. He moved forward, the gas cloud billowing.

There was a scream—a woman. Perhaps the queen or perhaps Bess or just a member of the household staff.

His leg paining him badly, the one-eyed man dropped the improvised cane. He'd need both hands.

He reached under his jacket, finding the butt of the Metalifed High Power with his left hand, wrenching it out of the Cobra rig. He thumbed back the hammer, one of the twenty-round magazines in place.

He looked at Mike O'Hara. "In case we die—I love you like a brother, Mike," Frost told him.

O'Hara—his eyes strange-looking behind the gas mask—touched Frost's left shoulder with his left hand. "Yeah—yeah, me, too, Hank."

Side by side they started into the royal apartments.

Frost turned a doorway, O'Hara stopping first, Frost lurching against the door frame for support.

It was Robert Walter, and in the center of the room, a man Frost recognized as Prince Philip wrestling on the floor with one of the legionnaires—it looked like the prince was winning. Other faces—faces he'd seen in newspapers were being held at gunpoint. And the queen—she dominated the room as she glared defiantly at Robert Walter, Bess struggling as Walter held her wrists in his left hand.

Frost shouted at the top of his lungs, ripping away the mask, the gas dissipated here, O'Hara edging to Frost's left, trying to cover the room, Frost knew.

"Walter—you son of a bitch. You'll never get out of here alive."

"I don't care—I'll have done what I bloody well set out

186

to do."

"You got my woman, you got my best friend's gun on the queen of England"—the Model 29 was leveled at her head—"and I'm gonna kill you dead right here and right now—before you can kill the queen, before you can get the job done."

"Shoot him," Walter shouted.

There was a burst of assault rifle fire from Frost's left. O'Hara, Frost knew.

Two of the legionnaires went down, a thin man—it was Prince Charles—straight-arming a third man in the face, snatching up an assault rifle. The queen's husband, Prince Philip, was up now, a Browning High Power in his right fist, aimed at Walter.

Frost shouted again. "You're dead. You're fuckin' dead, Walter."

He raised the High Power in his left hand—the right hand was too good for Walter—and aimed it at the center of Walter's forehead, between the eyes.

Walter started to thumb cock the 29, to kill the queen. Bess bit him in the left hand. Walter's eyes flickered. Frost squeezed the Metalifed High Power's trigger.

One shot—a neat hole between the eyes, the queen dodging left, away from the muzzle of the revolver.

A second shot, the head snapping back, the forehead spraying blood now like a spout.

A third shot, the head snapping back, Bess loose of Walter as the body started reeling.

A fourth shot. The right ear was gone. Frost wondered if Walter knew any good ear patch jokes.

A fifth shot—into the neck. He'd never hear Walter's voice again.

A sixth shot—the nose gone.

It was O'Hara shouting. "He's dead, Frost."

Frost lowered the High Power—Bess ran toward him. The gun still in his left fist—like he guessed it would always be in his fist—he folded the woman into his arms. "Bess."

"Frost," she whispered, and he heard her crying.

The gunfire from outside had stopped. Frost looked behind him for an instant, pushing aside a lock of Bess's blond hair in front of his eye. It was the old man in the air raid helmet. He cleared his throat, threw his shoulders back, then said, "Ma'am—your subjects have suppressed the threat."

Chapter Thirty-Two

The one-eyed man, his left leg out straight ahead of him in the back seat of the Rolls Royce, folded his left arm around Bess's shoulders, her shoulders bare under the fur stole she wore, the floor-length white gown making her look like a queen, Frost thought. More a princess as he looked at her green eyes.

O'Hara—Frost looked to his far left, past Bess—the FBI man looked handsome in an almost ludicrous sort of way in the tuxedo he wore. Frost had seen the bulge of the Model 29 under it earlier.

"Whatcha lookin' at?" O'Hara snapped.

"You in a tuxedo," Frost laughed.

"Hell, you don't look any better—just 'cause your eye patch's the same color. Leave me alone."

"All right, guys," Bess smiled, her voice the soft, throaty alto—he loved her voice.

"That was some evening, huh," Frost smiled, changing the subject.

"Yeah, sitting down to eat with the royal family—that was all right," O'Hara nodded. Frost moved his arm to

189

glance at the Rolex—it was midnight. He found his battered old Zippo, then found a Camel in the half-crumpled pack in his side pocket. He rolled the striking wheel under his thumb, punching the tip of the cigarette into the blue-yellow flame.

Frost inhaled the smoke deep into his lungs, then listened as Bess spoke. "It was something—I mean I never expected to dine with the queen. She's such a beautiful lady."

"Yeah," Frost agreed, exhaling the cloud of gray smoke. "But I gotta say, little what's-his-name was cute."

"You mean the prince's boy," O'Hara suggested.

"Yeah," and Frost turned to Bess, smiling. Her eyes smiled back. "One of these days, gotta make ourselves a little guy like that."

She hugged his left arm.

Frost just looked at her, then leant toward her, kissing her lips lightly.

O'Hara's voice. "Go ahead, Frost—I can stand it. Tell me how you lost your eye again. I could use a good laugh."

Bess's mouth pulled up at the corners, her lips thin, warm looking to him.

Without taking his eye off her, the one-eyed man—Hank Frost—began, "Well, it's not much of a story really. . . ."

GREAT BOOKS

E-BOOKS

AUDIOBOOKS

& MORE

Visit us today

www.speakingvolumes.us